La

"Brazill offers a series of amusing episodes filled with breezy banter in this offbeat slice of British noir."

—*Publishers Weekly*

"It's all here, everything you've come to expect from a Paul D. Brazill caper—the fast pace, the witty banter, the grim humour and the classic tunes—except this time he's REALLY outdone himself. Unlike the lament in the song the title takes its name from, Paul's best years are surely still ahead of him."

—Paul Heatley, author of *Fatboy*

"Paul D. Brazill is the Crown Prince of Noir. That's my opinion, granted, but I stand by it. For those who require proof, just pick up his latest novel, *Last Year's Man*, and it will be clear why I make that statement. All hail the crown prince!"

—Les Edgerton, author of *The Rapist*, *The Bitch*, *Just Like That* and others

"Brazill is brilliant, a unique voice which stands out from the crowd."

—Keith Nixon, author of the Solomon Gray books

LAST YEAR'S
MAN

PAUL D. BRAZILL

LAST YEAR'S MAN

ALL
DUE
RESPECT

All Due Respect
An imprint of Down & Out Books
3959 Van Dyke Rd, Ste. 265
Lutz, FL 33558
www.DownAndOutBooks.com

Edited by Chris Black and Chris Rhatigan
Cover design by JT Lindroos

ISBN: 1-946502-89-8
ISBN-13: 978-1-946502-89-6

To Nick Quantril

THE FIRST PART

I leaned against an oak tree and pissed into a plastic Pepsi bottle. It was a slow and painful process for sure, but what else was I to do? The new hypertension tablets the doctor had given me seemed to be doing the trick but they had one particularly annoying side effect: I was always getting caught short. And at the most inopportune moments, too. Well, it was either the drugs or it was my age. I was a kick in the arse off sixty, after all. It had to be expected.

The tree branches stretched like long bony fingers grasping towards the gibbous moon. A dog howled. Someone, somewhere laughed. I groaned with relief and closed my eyes as I pissed. A sharp breeze cut through me. I shivered and finished pissing, zipped up my fly and carefully fastened the bottle top, making sure not to spill any of the contents. I didn't want to leave any DNA.

With the bottle in my jacket pocket, I put my black, leather gloves back on and slowly walked across the garden towards the large house. My knees and my back had been bloody killing me all day. I stopped on the patio and took off my black ski mask to scratch my shaven head. I'd need to get some new cream from the quack. One thing after another, really. My eczema had been getting worse over the last few years and now my left elbow was aching in the damp autumn air. I sighed. No doubt about it, I felt my age these days. Still, getting old may have its faults but it beats the alternative.

I moved closer to the French windows. Like all the houses in Holland Park, this one was worth a pretty penny although the owner hadn't bothered to splash out on a decent home security system.

Gary Beachwell was inside the home, reclining on his sofa, talking into his smartphone. He was wearing a paisley silk robe open to reveal his flabby white body. I remembered that Gary had been such a svelte young thing when he'd written for *The Face* magazine in the early eighties. He'd been the doyen of the New Romantics. The Boswell of post-punk. But the good life had taken its toll on him and he had more recently earned the nickname Gary Beached Whale. I listened in through the open kitchen window.

'Tintin Quarantino?' said Gary. 'Oh, he's just Jim Jarmusch for thickos. He's like a Beavis and

Butthead version of John Luc Godard.'

He laughed loudly at his own joke, a habit that had always grated on me.

'Of course I could do with the bloody money,' said Gary. 'I'm bloody skint.'

Which was what I had been told. Gary's controversial views had been courted by the media for years. But the cacophonous din of internet trolls had all but drowned him out recently. They were obnoxious for free, after all. His novels were out of print, too, and he refused to lower himself to the grubby level of self-publishing or ebooks.

Myself, I thought Gary had squandered his talent anyway. He should have written more novels and screenplays instead of wasting his time on those crap current affairs columns he used to knock out for the tabloids and broadsheets alike.

I took out my lock picks and opened the French windows with ease. It was stiflingly hot as I stepped inside. A silent television screen showed *Celebrity Big Brother*, though I didn't recognise any of the alleged celebrities. Then again, I never did these days.

'Really? How much?' said Gary, grinning.

He licked his lips and struggled to sit upright. He grabbed his half-full glass of champagne and knocked back the contents.

The sounds of Roxy Music's 'In Every Dream Home a Heartache' eased from an expensive sound system. Bryan Ferry didn't know the half of it.

Gary didn't notice me as I stepped in front of him.

I pointed my Glock at him and coughed. Gary looked up. His mouth opened wide. He dropped his champagne flute and it spilled over the floor.

'What...what the fuck?' he said. 'Who the bloody hell are you?'

'It doesn't matter who I am, Gary. I'm merely the harbinger. The harbinger of bad tidings, as it were. Lee Hughes sent me to give you a message,' I said.

Gary struggled to sit upright.

'Who the fuck is Lee Hughes? I don't know anyone called Lee Hughes,' he said.

'Well you do, sort of. After a fashion. Six degrees of separation and all that,' I said.

'What?'

'Six degrees of separation. Like the film? We're all connected. We're all six steps away from each other and you, Gary, are six steps away from Lee Hughes. Lee is your Kevin Bacon, as it were.'

Gary started to sweat. He looked in pain. He farted.

'Yeah, I know what it is but I still don't know

what the bloody hell you're talking about,' he said.

I kept the gun pointed at him while I switched off the Roxy Music CD.

'Ah, but you do Gary,' I said. 'You really do.'

'But I don't...I don't know,' said Gary.

I sighed.

'Listen. Once upon a time,' I said, 'back in the early eighties, you had a brief but notorious period as a music journalist, did you or did you not?'

'Yeah. Yeah, I did.' He glanced over at the bottle of champagne. 'Can I have a drink?'

'Knock yourself out,' I said.

Gary picked up the bottle and downed its contents in one, dribbling. He closed his eyes and burped.

'Go on,' he said.

'Well, around that time there was a Mod revival. Bands like Secret Affair, The Chords, and The Purple Hearts. They did alright for themselves for a while. And one of those bands was a bunch of snotty nosed oiks called The Odds and Mods. Remember them?'

'Sort of.'

'You should. You reviewed their debut LP for the NME. You gave it a scathing, piss-taking review with the headline 'Like Lambrettas to the Slaughter'. Does that ring any bells?' I said.

'Yeah, now I remember. It was just a joke, really.

I quite liked the record but I couldn't admit to it.
My remit was to slag things off.'

'And that you did, Gary, that you did. You did it
very well, too, if I might say so. But one of the band
members, a bloke called Harry Hughes, the singer,
well, he really took that review to heart and to cut
a long story short, he ended up topping himself.
Threw himself into the Thames.'

'I didn't know. I mean, it was just a joke. I had
to—'

I held up a hand.

'As you say. But Harry Hughes' son, the afore-
mentioned Lee Hughes, has harboured a bit of a
grudge against you ever since,' I said. 'And in a
simple twist of fate, Lee recently won the lottery.
And, in a roundabout way, he subsequently hired
someone to hire me. To, well, to do this.'

I shot Gary in the chest. Twice to make sure and
once in the head just for luck. As was my want.

I put away my gun and took the Roxy Music CD
out of the player. I'd forgotten just how good *For
Your Pleasure* was. I was putting the CD back into
its case when I heard the scream.

The woman who stood in the doorway was
young, mid-twenties maybe. She wore a black
cocktail dress and an old, pink Sony Walkman. She
held a whip pointed at me.

'Get out,' she croaked.

I raised my Glock but the woman cracked the whip on my hand and I dropped the gun to the floor.

'Jesus!' I shouted. 'That bloody hurt.'

My back ached as I bent over to pick up my gun and by the time I'd straightened myself up, the woman was gone. A door slammed as I rushed into the hallway. I opened the front door and saw the woman trying to get into a red Mini Cooper. She was struggling to open the car door.

She dropped her keys and I raised my gun, pointed and fired twice, hitting her both times in the back. She slouched over the car, groaning. I walked across the pebbled driveway and shot her in the back of the head. She collapsed to the ground. I turned her over and saw that she was barely out of her teens. Practically a child. I closed her dead blue eyes.

'Oh bugger,' I said. 'Oh, bugger, oh, bugger, oh, bugger.'

An old advertising jingle corkscrewed my brain as I stripped to the waist in the morning dew and started to dig. With great effort, I hurled Gary Beachwell's flabby corpse into the grave then threw the young girl's body on top. I paused for a moment to evacuate my guts. When I was good and done I wiped my mouth on the back of my hand and picked up my thermos flask, took a swig of coffee and considered my predicament.

I'd always thought myself the consummate professional. My executions had always been short and sharp. The corpses were disposed of quickly and never discovered. There'd never been any witnesses and I never left a corpse to be discovered. I always cleaned the murder scene as if I'd never been there and I'd never killed an innocent bystander. No women, no children. Those were my rules. Until last night when it all went pear-shaped as quickly as spit disappears on a hot pavement. I was draped in a cloak of gloom and I was angry. Angry with myself. I picked up the shovel and started digging.

Sweating, I finished filling the grave and walked over to my Skoda. The frost-coated grass crackled beneath my heavy feet. I opened the car boot and wiped myself all over with one of the towels that I'd taken from Gary Beachwell's home.

I took out a clean shirt and put on my jacket. I wiped down the shovel and placed it back against the gravestone where I'd found it. There was nobody around but me and a chewed-up old ginger tomcat that crawled towards a rumbling mausoleum as if seeking sanctuary.

A church bell echoed through the granite winter morning as I got in the car. I listened to Pink Floyd's *Dark Side of The Moon* as I drove and before long a familiar feeling overwhelmed me. A sense of loss. The ache I felt lately wasn't just physical, that was for sure. The days were slipping through my fingers like grains of sand.

I awoke to the smell of coffee just after midday. It was the longest I'd slept for a long time even though the sleep had been fitful and cluttered with disturbing dreams. I still felt tired. The late nights, the job and its concurrent lifestyle were taking their toll to be sure. Like Danny Glover in *Lethal Weapon*, I was getting too old for this shit. I took a long and painful slash, showered and dressed as quickly as I could. As per usual, I went for the old duffer look: checked shirt, brown cords and cardigan, and half-moon glasses. I stuck two ballpoint pens in my shirt pocket for good measure. I knocked back a couple of painkillers with a bottle of Tracer Joe's coconut water. I left the door to the flat open for the cleaner and headed downstairs to The Bistro.

Alessio was behind the counter cleaning the La Spaziale coffee machine. It was a recent purchase of mine and the young Italian pretty much doted on it. In the corner, Greta was packing the vacuum cleaner away.

'Do you want me to do your flat today, Mr Bennett?' she said when she saw me.

'Yes, please Greta.'

She nodded and headed up the stairs. I had tried to get her to call me Tommy when she started to work for me but she'd said that wasn't the Lithuanian way. I was her boss and her senior so I would always be Mr Bennett to her. Greta was barely forty but she was much more conservative than a lot of British women of that age. She was divorced with two teenage sons who were built like brick shithouses and doted on their mother.

The Bistro had just opened but there was already a customer. A tall, blonde woman in an expensive black suit and large framed glasses. She tapped away at an iPad and sipped her cappuccino.

I took the previous night's *Evening Standard* from the counter and sat near the window. I flicked through the newspaper with little interest.

'Brekkie, Mr B?' said Alessio.

'Yes, please son,' I said.

Alessio smiled and nodded towards the young woman in the corner, winking. Unlike Greta, Alessio behaved a lot younger than his age. Twenty going on twelve, in fact.

'Do you want music?' said Alessio.

A radio was playing twenty-four-hour news in Italian. Although I understood a little of the lingo, I rarely listened to the news these days. It always made me depressed and I wasn't a masochist. Life really was too short for all that.

'Yes, that would be nice. In fact, there's a new CD on the machine,' I said.

Alessio picked up the Roxy Music CD and squinted at the cover.

'Let me guess, you've never heard of them,' I said.

'And you're right,' said Alessio. 'Nice lady on the cover, though.'

He kissed it.

I resisted the temptation to tell him that Amanda Lear, *For Your Pleasure's* cover model, used to be a man. Like Greta, Alessio was also a tad conservative. They'd both been with me since I'd opened The Bistro a few years before and they'd never let me down. Alessio's dad, Paolo DeLuca, was an old business acquaintance of mine who wanted his son to have a normal job, at least for a while. I tried my best to keep Alessio out of trouble and I usually succeeded though the lad did have quite an eye for the ladies, which had got him into the odd scrape. I had met Greta when I took a shortcut down an alleyway in Acton almost twenty years before and found a couple of Russian thugs trying to knock her about. She was giving as good as she got, mind you, but I stepped in and sorted things out when I saw that she was pregnant. When I opened The Bistro, I needed someone I could trust to do the cleaning and odd jobs. Someone who could handle themselves if things went pear-shaped. Greta ticked all the right boxes. She owned her own cleaning firm but refused to let any of her staff clean The Bistro or my flat.

Alessio brought over my coffee, orange juice and pain au chocolate as Roxy Music's 'Do the Strand' kicked out. He danced back behind the counter and I stared out at Chiswick High Road. The traffic was slow due to the inevitable roadworks on Kings Street but people were still rushing about as usual. Everybody talking into or staring at their phones. None of them seemed aware of what was going on around them. They were trapped in their own bubbles of self-importance.

I was watching a traffic warden argue with a man in a Santa costume when the young woman in black got up from her seat and sat down next to me.

'The traffic warden doesn't have a lot of the

Christmas spirit, I think,' she said.

'Well, it's only November,' I said. 'And by the looks of him old Santa has had more than enough spirits.'

She smiled. 'I'm Magda,' she said.

She held out a perfectly manicured hand. I shook it.

'Jeff Munday requested that I tell you that the remainder of your payment has been made in full,' she said.

I nodded. 'And?'

'And?' she said.

'Well, Mr Munday didn't need to send you to tell me he'd paid me. I checked my account last night. So, there must be something else.'

'Ah, yes,' she said. 'There is.'

She looked out of the window. She looked embarrassed, flustered.

'I...may require your services,' she said.

Her English was perfect but I noticed the slight trace of an Eastern European accent.

'As Mr Munday probably told you,' I said, 'I'm pretty much retired now. I'm getting a bit long in the tooth. The job for Jeff was as much a favour as anything else. His old mum put me up when I first moved down here to London from the frozen wastelands of the north. I owe her and her family a lot.'

'I know, he told me.'

'Did he?'

'Yes, he did.'

'Does he tell you a lot?'

'Quite a lot. You see, I'm his psychologist.'

'Oh, how very Tony Soprano,' I said.

Magda smiled.

I chuckled as Santa Claus threw a punch at the traffic warden who avoided it easily and stepped back to let Father Christmas fall forward and crash to the ground.

'Perhaps we could discuss my situation and decide,' said Magda. 'I'll pay you what you wish.'

'Maybe,' I said. 'Though trust is the main issue in my game. I've been burnt a few times in the past. I'll check with Jeff and see if he vouches for you.'

'Perhaps you could come to see me as a client? Then I would be bound by doctor patient confidentiality. Anything we discussed would be between you and me.'

I sighed and scratched my head.

'Oh, why not?' I said. 'People have been telling me that I need a check-up from the neck up for years. I tell you what, I'll think about it.'

She nodded and handed me a business card.

'Phone me when or if you are ready,' she said.

She smiled and got up.

'Goodbye Mr B,' she said and left The Bistro.

She seemed oblivious as an ambulance mounted the pavement near her and two paramedics jumped out and ran towards Father Christmas.

I went back to reading the newspaper. There was a report about Alice Cooper finding an Andy Warhol painting that he'd forgotten he had for fifteen years. Worth millions, apparently. I turned over the page and saw that George Clooney was suing a French tabloid for publishing photos of his kids. Angelina Jolie was sick again.

As I sat and finished my breakfast, I watched dark clouds spread across the sky like a cancer. A man in a black hoodie stood across the road staring into The Bistro. He looked familiar. I shuddered and rubbed my eyes. I opened them again and he was gone.

I got up and put on my black overcoat. I checked my pockets. Wallet, mobile phone, keys, gun. All the essentials.

'Thanks for that, Alessio,' I said. 'I'm just popping down to the supermarket for a few supplies. Is there anything I can get you?'

'No thank you. I think we have everything,' said Alessio.

He glanced out the window as a tall bottle-blonde who was better dressed for summer than autumn walked past.

'See you in a bit,' I said.

Alessio grunted something. I put on my Homberg hat and left.

Chiswick High Road was full of people collecting for charities, as usual. Like running the gauntlet of rattling tins and smug, accusing faces. I was almost outside Sainsbury's when I heard a loud bang. Self-preservation immediately took over as I stepped back into a pub doorway and watched the chaos. Sirens howled and people screamed. Children cried and dogs barked.

The police and ambulance were there in seconds. A gangling hipster that frequented The Bistro holding a tissue to his red face. I went into the pub. Most people were looking out the window but the barflies were still hanging around the bar, their attention barely scuffed by the commotion outside.

'What can I get you?' said a chubby barman with a bum-fluff moustache.

'I'll have a mineral water, please,' I said.

'Fizzy or still?'

'Still.'

'Ice and a slice?'

'No ta. Just the water. Any idea what the bang was about? Terrorists again?'

The barman shrugged.

'Maybe,' he said. 'Though there are those that have their own ideas, eh?'

He nodded toward a prune-faced old man who was slouched over the bar protecting his glass of whiskey.

'It was The Mardi Gras Experience, I reckon,' said Walter.

'What's that, then, Walt?' I said.

'You're not local are you?' he said.

'I am now,' I said.

'Yeah, but you weren't born and bred here like me. How long have you lived in Chiswick?'

'About fifteen years,' I said.

'Ah, well you would have missed the first Mardi Gras Experience then,' said Walter.

The barman gave me my drink and I paid.

'I most certainly did,' I said. 'What was it?'

The old bloke necked his drink and smiled at me. 'Buy me a drink and I'll tell you.'

I laughed and nodded to the barman.

'Get him what he wants,' I said.

'Double or single?' said the barman.

'Make it a double,' I said. 'I have a feeling this could be a long story.'

The barman poured the drinks. Walter took a sip.

'Well, you see, back in the nineties,' he said, 'there

was a bloke called Edgar Pearce. He lived locally and was a bit of a nutter. He was a friend of a friend, like. Used to drink in this here pub, from time to time. They said he suffered from something called Binswanger's disease.'

'Never heard of it.'

'Few have. Anyway, he was an extortionist and he planted bombs in Barclay's Bank, Sainsbury's and a couple of other places. He even stalked customers and staff. He threatened to shoot them with a crossbow!'

'Sounds like a real fruit loop. What's the Mardi Gras connection, then?'

'Well, he used to leave calling cards saying, 'Welcome to the Mardi Gras Experience' at the places he blew up. He's still a bit of a local legend.'

'And you actually reckon this is him?' I said.

'Nah, can't be. Pearce is still in the slammer,' said Walter.

He tapped the side of his nose.

'But, you know, it could be one of those copy-cats, like. You never know. I tell you, London's a risky place, these days.'

I chuckled.

'It is indeed. I'll have to shop at Marks and Spencer's while Sainsbury's is closed and those prices are lethal!' I said.

We both laughed. I finished my drink.

'See you later, Walter,' I said, and left the pub.

The band in The Packhorse and Talbot really were doing my napper in. A bunch of saggy has-beens were knocking out some painful, horrible hybrid of blues rock and folk rock. Even the few songs that I liked were mangled into some sort of plodding anonymity. 'Whiskey in the Jar'. 'Born to Run'. 'Brass in Pocket'. They all sounded the bloody same. The singer wasn't too bad but he seemed to fancy himself as Jim Morrison and he really was far too old for those leather trousers. The crowd seemed to be lapping it up, though. A bunch of sweaty, middle-aged men in supermarket jeans. When the singer started moaning about how, if it wasn't for bad luck he'd have no luck at all, I finished my Diet Coke and left.

As I walked down to Turnham Green tube station, my mind was heavy with doubts.

When I arrived at The French House it was stuffed and stuffy. The Fox twins, Chloe and Adele, were leaning against an open window drinking prosecco. The twins were professional criminals. Burglars and safe-crackers, for the most part. Sometimes smugglers. I'd known them since I first stumbled, tumbled and tripped into London. They were both dressed head to toe in black, as always.

'Evening,' I said.

'Cheers Mr B,' said Adele. 'What brings you downtown?'

'I just fancied a change. I needed to wash the cobwebs away,' I said.

I sipped my espresso.

'Well, you're just in time for one of Adele's rants,' said Chloe. 'Lucky you.'

Adele rolled her eyes. 'I was just expressing an opinion.'

'Express away,' I said.

'So. The things that I like about the French House are,' said Adele. She counted off on her long fingers. 'The wine, the food, the location, the lack of shite music. Oh, and that people can't use mobile bloody phones. The things I don't like: it's always full on a Friday night and full of media tossers at that.'

She took a swig of her drink.

'But you still come here,' said Chloe. 'Week after week...'

'Oh, I love it. You know that. It's part of Soho history. Francis Bacon, Derek Raymond. Real London. Well, the London we all fled the sticks to escape to, anyway,' said Adele.

I nodded.

Adele scraped away at her black nail varnish. It flaked off easily.

'The world turns,' I said.

'*Vive le difference!*' said Chloe.

'*Oui! Oui!*' said Adele.

'Oh, don't start that again! I've just been for a slash and the queue for the toilets was bloody torture,' I said.

Adele took out an e-cigarette.

'Maybe we should all piss off for a bit. We could go somewhere more bohemian, like Barcelona or Prague. Even New York. You always wanted to go to CBGB,' said Adele.

'I very much doubt it's still there. It's probably a Starbucks now,' I said. 'Selling decaffeinated latte with skimmed milk.'

'Oh, you know what I mean!' said Chloe.

'I do,' I said. 'I do indeed.'

I thought for a moment, biting my bottom lip. I stared out of the window. A group of city boys staggered down Dean Street singing an Ed Sheeran song.

'Oh dear,' said Adele. 'Maybe leaving London isn't such a bad idea.'

The city boys started giving each other piggy backs. I shook my head.

'It's enough to turn a man to drink, it really is,' I said.

'Do you think they know how ridiculous they are?' said Adele.

'I doubt it,' I said. 'The most ridiculous people are usually those that don't know just how ridiculous they are.'

'As opposed to The Madeley Syndrome,' said Chloe.

'What's that?'

'It's when you're just about clever enough to know how stupid you are,' said Chloe. 'But not clever enough to do anything about it.'

'It's named after the television presenter Richard Madeley,' said Adele, grinning.

'Makes sense,' I said.

We were silent as we watched a woman dressed as Paddington bear, holding the head under one of her arms, stagger past the pub blowing a kazoo.

'I think I'd miss that if I left Blighty,' I said. 'The daftness.'

'Oh, I'm sure you could find daftness wherever you went,' said Adele.

'Yes, like attracts like,' said Chloe.

'Thanks for the vote of confidence, lasses,' I said.

THE SECOND PART

There was a time when Knightsbridge was full of Arabs. When the streets were cluttered with Saudi princes and their wives. These days, however, you needed to be able to speak Russian just to order a cup of tea. I was sat in the Paxton's Head drinking Earl Grey. I'd wanted to go to The Tea Clipper on Montpellier Street but it was still closed. Apparently, its new owners had wanted to turn it into a house but it was a listed building and planning permission was refused. The Paxton's Head was even older than The Tea Clipper, mind you. It had been built in 1632. A true piece of London history and it hadn't changed much since I'd last been in. So much of London had changed, though, since I'd first arrived broke and homeless back in the early eighties.

In fact, I'd been thinking of selling up and moving on a lot lately. Maybe to sunny Spain. Or Thailand. An old crony of mine owned a bar in Bangkok and seemed to be having a good enough time of it. He was always on at me to head over to see him and it did seem tempting. London was losing its lustre for sure. As if on cue, it started to rain and the music changed to the theme from *Friends*. Gloomily, I sat and drank my tea as a group of irate Japanese tourists dressed as Sherlock Holmes rushed into the pub to shelter from the downpour.

It was still raining as I left the Paxton's Head and walked to Dr Magdalena Nowak's clinic on Lower Sloane Street. I'd neglected to take an umbrella but I did have the black Homberg hat which matched my black overcoat nicely and protected me from the elements. A tall man in a long black raincoat stood in the rain beneath a blinking streetlamp. He nodded at me as I passed but I tried to ignore him. To pretend he wasn't there. When I looked back, he was gone.

Magda's clinic was in a converted nineteenth-century Pont Street Dutch-style redbrick house, so it was pretty safe to say she wasn't short of a bob or two.

I was about to ring the doorbell when the front door opened.

'I'm glad you could make it,' said Magda. 'I've

cancelled all of my appointments for today. Come on in.'

I walked into the hallway and looked around. I whistled.

'Swanky pad you've got here, doc,' I said.

'I rent,' she said, as if to end the topic.

The hallway was filled with Muzak—sleepy synthesizers and yawning saxophones. The pastel walls were covered with generic abstract paintings—all splashes, dots and sharp lines—that were probably worth a fortune.

'Let's go into my office,' she said.

Magda's office was typically anonymous. Just like every headshrinker's office I'd ever seen in films or on the telly. So neutral as to be positively without personality.

'Do I take a seat or the sofa?' I said.

'Sit wherever you feel comfortable. I take it you have spoken to Jeff Munday and he vouched for me?'

'I have and he did.'

I sat in a leather armchair.

'Would you like a tea or coffee?' said Magda. 'Or maybe water?'

'No thanks. I'm trying to limit my caffeine intake,' I said.

'Good for you but you should drink water. Two

litres a day is recommended.'

I shrugged. She was probably right but if I did that I'd never be out of the toilet.

'Maybe a glass of wine? It's after noon,' she said.

'No ta. I've been off the sauce for more than ten years now. No booze or red meat, in fact.'

'Do you smoke?'

'Just the odd cigar at Christmas and the like,' I said.

'Very good,' said Magda. 'You don't mind if I imbibe, do you?'

'Not a problem.'

She poured a large glass of burgundy and took a sip. Then another.

'Okay. I'll get down to business,' she said. 'Are you familiar with the Bailey family?'

'I know a few Baileys but if it's the family I think you're referring to, then yes. The Baileys are one of London's most formidable criminal gangs and a very nasty bunch they are too. Especially these days. They were always a bit heavy handed but since old Ma Bailey croaked it, they've really crossed over into the dark side.'

'Indeed.'

She took a swig of wine.

'That's the thing,' she said. 'You see, when I first came to London—from Poland, back in the nineties—

I had no money and no job. And in a roundabout way, I became a hostess at one of the Bailey family's...entertainment emporiums.'

'Needs must,' I said. 'I was living on the streets and begging until Jeff Munday's mam took me in. London's a great city but it's not easy to survive unless you have money.'

'Yes, well, survive I did. I worked and saved. I put myself through school and became a psychologist. And I thought I'd left my past behind. Until recently.'

She rubbed the back of her neck.

'So, let me guess. You're being blackmailed by the Bailey family.'

'Correct. The Baileys filmed all of my meetings with clients.'

'So, what are they after, money?'

'No. They want information. Damaging information on my current clients. At least my powerful and influential ones.'

I closed my eyes and rubbed them.

'So, what do you want from me?' I said. 'Which of the Baileys is the big threat? Which one shall I erase?'

Magda leant forward. Her eyes twinkled.

'Oh, Mr B, I want you to kill them all. Slaughter every single fucking one of the bastards.'

I laughed. 'You don't do things by half, do you?'

'I am a big believer in closure.'

She leant back and folded her arms.

'So, will you take the job?' she said.

'It'll cost you, but for sure I'll do it. I never liked the Baileys, anyway.'

She smiled. 'Good. Very good.'

She took another swig of wine. She looked flushed.

'Could I use your toilet?' I said.

'Of course. It's there,' she said.

Magda pointed to a door. I went in and had a tinkle. When I got back, she'd almost finished off the bottle of wine and seemed a tad tipsy.

'While you're here, is there anything I can help you with?' she said.

I sat down.

'Well, maybe,' I said. 'You see, I've been having these dreams.'

'Bad dreams?' she said.

'Oh, yes,' I said. 'Very bad, indeed.'

'Tell me more.'

'This may sound daft but...do you believe in ghosts?'

I sat on a bench in the darkened park and watched the Bailey boys get out of their Daimler. I was dressed head to foot in black and holding a black briefcase. The Baileys walked up to The Black Cat Casino and opened the front door with a key.

The Baileys were bad people, for sure. Drug dealing, loan sharking, money laundering, people trafficking. They had their grubby fingers in so many dirty pies. But they had friends in high places. Power and influence. So they remained untouchable by the law for a very long time.

They were also creatures of narrow habit. Come rain or shine, hell or high water, each Monday, just after midnight, the boys visited their casino to talk business with their sister. One hour later, they all got into the Daimler and returned home.

I waited for fifty-five minutes and crossed the road to the car. I took the Semtex out of the briefcase and strapped it under the car. The sciatica in my back and knee hurt as I bent and stood up again. I massaged my joints. Then I needed a piss.

I stood in the shadows of a closed down Methodist church having a slash when I heard the bang. I finished and went to look at my handiwork.

The orange and crimson flames licked the night sky. Smoke billowed. The car was ablaze. Sirens screamed in the distance but I decided to wait and watch.

I smirked as I saw Detective Sergeant Ronnie

Burke get out of his car and stand close to the flames and try to get some warmth. Burke was dressed as a schoolboy and holding a blow-up guitar. Detective Inspector Niki Scrace laughed as she walked towards Ronnie. Her red hair was tied back tightly and she wore a black raincoat over her black trouser suit. I moved closer, keeping to the shadows.

'Now, either you were at the Essex Arms' fancy-dress karaoke tonight when you got the call,' said Niki, 'or you're having a major mid-life crisis. And knowing you, I suspect the latter.'

Ronnie took a school cap from his pocket and put it on his dyed black hair.

'Can't you guess who I'm supposed to be?' he said.

'Don't tempt me,' said Niki.

Ronnie started to sing AC/DC's 'Highway to Hell'.

'Yes, yes, I do get it,' said Niki. 'So what's going on here? Why have you dragged me out of my *Game of Thrones* binge to stand in the cold in bloody Acton. You know I bloody hate bloody Acton.'

'I don't have a lot of information but here's the person who called it in. She might have more details,' said Ronnie.

Detective Sergeant Jola Lach walked towards them. She was dressed identically to Niki but her blonde hair was cropped short. They looked like a lesbian couple, which was apparently what they were, though I'd heard a rumour that Jola once had a fling with Ronnie. The police force was as tangled a web as it had always been.

'What's the story morning glory?' said Ronnie.

'A couple of the undercover boys were staking out the casino,' said Jola. Her Polish accent had been smoothed since she'd moved to London. 'They were hanging around in the all-night café opposite.' She pointed towards Madge's Café.

'What exactly were they looking out for?' said Niki.

'The Black Cat Casino is owned by the Bailey gang and our boys had a tip off that they were using it to launder money from arms smuggling.'

'Ah, the lovely Bailey gang. I'd been wondering what they were up to,' said Niki.

'Yep, we haven't heard so much as a squeak from them since the Robinson gang blew their mother to bits,' said Ronnie.

'Allegedly,' said Niki.

'Oh, yes. But not very allegedly,' said Ronnie.

'So, why did you call us?' said Niki. 'We're the murder squad. Arms dealing isn't our thing.'

'This is more off the record,' said Jola. 'One of the undercover boys spotted a friend of yours leaving the casino and getting into the car with the Bailey family.'

'And who might that be?' said Ronnie.

'I'm sorry,' said Jola. 'But it was Lee. Detective Sergeant Lee Winspear.'

'Christ!' said Ronnie.

Oh, shit, I thought. A dead copper. Now I really was so far up shit creek that an outdoor motor wouldn't help me, let alone a paddle.

The Bistro hadn't yet opened when I went downstairs, and the lights were still switched off. Greta stood outside smoking a menthol cigarette and Alessio was sat at a table near the window, rubbing his red eyes and reading a copy of *Shoot*. He looked surprised to see me.

'You're up early, Mr B,' he said.

He stood.

'Sit back down, son,' I said. 'Let's wait for Greta. I want to have a word with you both.'

'Sounds serious,' he said,

'It is.'

'Is this good news or bad news?' he said.

'Well that, as they say, is simply a matter of perspective,' I said, as Greta came into The Bistro.

* * *

It was midday when I left The Bistro and walked on to Chiswick High Road. I flagged down a passing taxi.

'Dead centre of town,' said the taxi driver when I told him where I wanted to go.

He dropped me off outside Kensal Green Cemetery's wrought-iron gates and I walked through the rain towards Kate's grave. I placed a bottle of London Pride on the grave. My wife hated flowers because of her hay fever. I leaned against the headstone.

'I won't ask how you are,' I said. 'Being a tad redundant and all that but I do have some news. I tell you Kate, at the moment I feel like a cowboy in some old film. Staked out in the desert and watching the vultures circle above me. So, I've decided to leave London. To go abroad for a bit. Who'd have thought it, eh?'

It started to rain and I was without an umbrella again. I waited for a few moments, as if awaiting a reply, gave her a nod as if she had, then headed off towards the bus stop. A large fat man dressed in black stood beneath a tree, laughing soundlessly.

* * *

I walked into Gordon's Wine Bar, down the narrow staircase, and stooped as I entered the dark cellar. The place smelled of wine and cheese. Full of after-work drinkers, tourists and bright young things. Flashy media types and city boys sat around chatting. Magda sat at a rickety candle-lit table drinking a glass of Gordon's Veneto Red. She was reading a Kindle.

I sat opposite. She smiled.

'I was just reading the *Evening Standard*,' she said. 'It seems as if the Bailey family are no more. Is it true?'

'Yes, I managed to eradicate all of them in one fell swoop. Unfortunately, I also croaked a copper so bent that you could use him as a pipe cleaner,' I said.

'I don't understand,' she said.

'There was a policeman in the car with them,' I said.

'Really? It says nothing of this in the newspaper.'

'I know, that's what worries me,' I said.

It also worried me that there were undercover police watching The Black Cat Casino who must have seen me plant the bomb under the Baileys' car. I really was losing my touch not to have spotted them.

A handsome West African waiter came over to the table.

'Can I get you something to drink, sir,' he said in a cut-glass accent sharp enough to shave with.

'An espresso, please,' I said. 'I need it today.'

I hadn't slept a wink all night. I'd been waiting for the boys in blue to knock at my door, or kick it in, and now felt much more uneasy that they hadn't.

When the waiter went away, I leaned forward.

'The thing is, I'm going to bugger off for a while,' I said. 'Let the blip disappear from the radar. Lay low. Keep my head down. Head off to foreign lands.'

'What are you going to do about The Bistro?' said Magda.

'I'll leave it in Greta's safe hands. She'll have her sons help out if there are any problematic customers. And I've promised Alessio that he can employ an understudy. Probably a pretty young girl, knowing him, but Greta will keep an eye on him. Make sure he doesn't get too hands on with his training.'

Magda smiled.

The waiter brought my coffee.

'Thanks,' I said.

'I have your money,' said Magda, when the waiter went away. 'In cash as you requested.'

She slid a large stainless-steel briefcase under the table to me.

I'd thought it best to have some walking around

35

money. Just in case the police froze my bank accounts. I really didn't know what was going on or what I'd got myself involved in. Luckily, I had a decent fake passport back at my flat so I could be out of the country in no time at all.

'Thanks,' I said, as I put the briefcase under my chair.

'How will you get such a large amount out of the country?' she said.

'I have my ways.'

'Then the world is your oyster.'

'Yeah, but I'm a vegetarian,' I said.

I was losing my touch. Maybe I had been for some time and hadn't realised it. I got off the tube at Stamford Brook and walked onto King Street. I was so deep in thought that I didn't notice the black BMW until it pulled up next to me.

The driver's window wound down.

'Get in, Mr B,' said a familiar face, full of false joviality. 'We need to have a word.'

With Sisyphean resignation, I got in the car.

My hot breath appeared and disappeared on the cold windowpane like a spectre. I couldn't help smiling as I watched a bunch of kids playing football in the park outside. A big dog barked at them while an old woman drank coffee from a tartan thermos. The kids waved to her and headed off across the park. A man in black stepped out of the trees and waved to me. I turned away.

'I'll just put that there for safekeeping,' I said, putting my gun on the table.

Bernie shrugged and grunted. As annoying as ever.

I had been doing my best to keep calm, I really had. But it was hard there in that room. The cold didn't help. I had turned up the collar on my coat and put my hat and leather gloves back on, but I was still freezing my balls off.

Detective Inspector Bernie Clarke, on the other hand, had taken off his jacket, loosened his tie and rolled up his sleeves. Looking like a reject from *Miami Vice* in his powder blue linen suit and salmon pink shirt, he was knocking back the Evian and dabbing his forehead with a paper towel. Semi circles of sweat around each armpit.

I stamped my feet on the concrete floor.

Bernie snorted. He walked over to a globe-shaped drinks cabinet in the corner of the half-decorated office and opened it up. This was the office Bernie used for what he called his extra-curricular meetings.

The discussions that he didn't want his colleagues to know about. The dodgy stuff, basically.

'Too late for a snifter? Or too early?' he said. 'Or are you still on the wagon?'

I sighed and glanced towards the window. Two men in black stood in the park watching me.

'Oh, why not,' I said. 'It might warm me up.'

Bernie grinned and made himself a gin and tonic. He poured me a double Maker's Mark.

'I take it you won't be wanting ice,' he said.

He guffawed as he passed the drink to me. I took a sip. Then a gulp. It had been a while. I let the booze and the resignation wash over me.

'You're a droll fucker, Bernie,' I said. 'Always have been. Even when you were just a plod you were a lippy twat.'

He took a long, slow drink.

There was a loud bang against the office door and it slowly creaked open, scraping against the wooden floor.

'Speak of the devil,' said Bernie.

Scarecrow shuffled into the room. His eyes and nose were red. He was tall, wiry. Had a dishevelled beard and wore a crumpled charity shop tweed suit. Scuffed brogues. Still, since he was an undercover copper—and had been as long as I could remember—the scarecrow look worked well for him.

'Jesus, Scarecrow, you look like shite. Even by your low standards,' I said.

Scarecrow plucked a pin-sized roll up from his bottom lip. Smirked.

'I've seen better days, aye,' he rasped. 'But I haven't had better nights, I can tell you.'

He winked and collapsed into a leather armchair still covered in cellophane. Held out a hand, clicked his fingers.

Bernie frowned, went to the mini-bar and filled a half pint glass with vodka. He handed it to Scarecrow, who took a swig. Licked his lips.

'Breakfast of champions,' I said.

Scarecrow looked me up and down.

'Pots and kettles?' he said.

I looked at the half empty glass of whiskey in my hand. 'When in Rome,' I said.

Bernie topped up my glass.

'Here's a bit more spaghetti,' he said.

I sighed as I sat down on the edge of Bernie's desk.

'So, what's this all about then?' I said.

'Patience is a virtue, Tommy,' said Scarecrow. 'You should try to be a bit more zen. It'll help your blood pressure.'

'I'll stick your zen up your arse,' I said.

'I'd like to see you try, has-been.'

'Scarecrow!' barked Bernie. He got to his feet. 'Stop pissing about. We've got business to attend to.'

Scarecrow licked his ragged moustache. 'Alright, alright. Hold your arses.'

He carefully put his glass on the floor and unsteadily stood up. Made a show of stretching his muscles.

I chewed the inside of my cheek.

Scarecrow pushed a hand into his jacket inside pocket. Plucked out a small brown envelope and held it aloft.

'Ta dah! Viola, cello, banjo, whatever tickles your fancy,' he said.

He handed an envelope to me.

'What the hell is this?' I said.

'It's your next contract,' said Bernie.

'I told you, I'm retiring,' I said. 'Especially from working with you lot.'

Scarecrow chuckled. 'As if you have a choice,' he said. 'I have some nice footage of you sticking Semtex under the Bailey gang's car. Not that they'll be missed, of course. But a cop killer is still a cop killer.'

'I see,' I said. 'And I suspect I won't be getting paid for this job, either.'

'You guessed correctly,' said Scarecrow. 'We just

want to keep you busy for a bit.'

'And don't I know it,' I said. 'No peace for the wicked.'

'Still, we all have our own double-cross to bear,' I said. I grabbed my gun from the table and quickly blasted Scarecrow and Bernie in the face. I kept shooting until the gun was empty and went over to the window. There seemed to be even more phantoms in the rain-soaked park, all dressed in black and looking towards me. I picked up the bottle of whiskey and took a big swig. The spectres were gone. Maybe they were gone for good or maybe they'd return. I didn't know. But as I looked at the blood-splattered corpses on the floor, I knew I had to get out of London. And bloody sharpish, too.

THE THIRD PART

I woke up when someone stabbed me.

A snotty-nosed little girl dressed as Zorro was using a black plastic sword to prod me in the stomach. Her mask was askew and her hat was battered. She looked a little like one of my sister's kids—Kelly, Kaylee, Kelsey, Courtney or whatever—I really couldn't keep track of them all these days. Seemed to be a new one popping out every week. Coming into the world kicking and screaming, pretty much staying that way.

'Stand and deliver,' said the kid, grinning.

I looked around. The rest of the train's few passengers were sleeping or staring at their smartphones and tablets. Or perhaps they were just trying to ignore the little brat. My left leg was numb, as were my buttocks. I shuffled in my seat, stretched and yawned. My mouth was arid. I was hungover from bad booze, bad dreams and worse memories.

'And what exactly would you like me to deliver?' I croaked.

I cleared my throat.

'Deliver and de onions,' she said.

She laughed.

I forced a smile.

'That's very funny,' I said.

'I know. What's your name?' she said.

'Tommy,' I said.

'My cousin's called Tommy. He's a teacher. Are you a teacher? You look like my RE teacher. He has glasses, too. But he's fatter than you and he sweats a lot.'

'No, I'm not a teacher.'

'You don't dress like a teacher. You look like a priest.'

I looked down at my black shirt and suit. 'You're right at that.'

'Are you a priest?' she said.

I tapped the side of my nose. 'That's my secret.'

'Have you been to London?' she said.

'I have.'

'Did you see the Queen?'

'No, she was out when I called round. They said she was down the betting shop,' I said.

The girl grimaced. 'Where are you going now?'

'To Seatown,' I said.

'Why are you going there? My dad said it's a dump and full of thickos,' she said.

I shrugged. 'It's not so bad, really,' I said. 'I suppose I'm used to it. Mind you, I was born there, though I haven't been back for a while.'

'Why are you going?'

'I just fancied a change. And to see my mother.'

'How old is she?'

'She's eighty-nine.'

'Wow! Why doesn't she live with you?'

'Well, we don't really get on. And I can't take care of her.'

'Have you got any kids?'

'Yes, I've a daughter. She still lives in Seatown.'

'Is she a priest?'

'No, she's a teacher. An art teacher.'

My head started to hurt. Thinking and talking at the same time was too difficult that early in the day. I was never one to multitask. I massaged my temples. The girl giggled.

'What's your name?' I said.

'Mind your own business, you nonce,' she said.

She stuck her tongue out and ran off laughing.

I sighed and thought about the dream I'd just had. I was immediately draped in a dark cloak of gloom. I dug a can of Stella from my backpack, opened it and took a long swig. Then another. I leaned against the train window, closed my eyes and let the womb of booze smother me.

The carriage shook like a junkie in rehab and dragged me painfully awake. I looked out the window at Seatown train station and suddenly felt very cold. It wasn't the most inviting of places at the best of times. Still, at least the graffiti was new.

I stood and put on my coat. I picked up my suitcase and stiffly got off the long, black train. As I walked down the platform, I could see the little girl in the Zorro costume chasing an older girl who was dressed as a unicorn.

My bladder was full and felt ready to burst so I went to the public toilet but there was already a queue of smack heads shuffling about inside. I walked out of the station to look for the nearest pub. Seatown had changed for sure. Pubs had been renovated and given new names. New pubs had been given the names of old pubs. Fish and chip shops that had been turned into kebab shops were now fish and chip shops again. A church had been converted into an art gallery. The statue of an old civic dignitary in the middle of the road still had a road cone on its head, however. And the remnants of a Chinese takeaway in its outstretched hand. The church clock struck thirteen as I crossed the road.

A shiny black BMW with blacked out windows blocked the pedestrian crossing. I walked around the car and heard a hissing sound as one of the windows was wound down. I turned and saw a bony man with a long back ponytail staring at me. He looked as if he had on red lipstick and white face paint. He smiled, put a black cigarette in his mouth and lit it. I hadn't seen Drella for years. He had been a small-time enforcer when I last lived in Seatown but I'd heard he'd since skewered his way up the ranks of the town's underworld.

I rushed into the first pub I saw, The Tap and Spile, which I remembered had been inevitably nick-named The Spinal Tap back in the good-old-bad-old days.

I pushed my way through the crowd to the bar. Everyone seemed to have luggage of some sort. Suit-cases, backpacks and holdalls cluttered the sticky wooden floor. A big screen television was silently showing a rugby match though no one was watch-ing it. The Stone Roses blasted out. It had been renovated since the last time I'd been in but it was still a dump.

'What can I get you?' said the barmaid.

She was short, with dyed blonde hair and a nose piercing. She had a sharp Spanish accent and a sharper scowl. Her name tag said her name was Aneta.

'A pint of Guinness please,' I said. 'And where are the gents' toilets these days?'

She pointed to a graffiti-stained metal door at the end of the bar.

I nodded and heaved my suitcase into the graffiti-splattered toilet with me.

An old, wire-haired man leaned unsteadily against the wall, smoking a roll up. He squinted at me.

'It's a good life if you don't weaken,' he said, and left, his flies still wide open.

I tried the cubicles but they were all locked so I leaned my suitcase against a rusty radiator and pissed into a cracked urinal, relived that I hadn't needed a crap.

As I was washing my hands, the door opened and a ratty-looking man dressed in denim came in sniffing. He was wearing bright white Adidas trainers. His eyes and nose were red.

He marched around the room as if he were looking for something or someone and tried a cubicle door.

'They're both locked, mate,' I said, drying my hands on a paper towel.

'I'm not your frigging mate,' he said, in a ragged local accent.

He sniffed loudly and kicked one of the cubicle doors open. Empty. He kicked another door open revealing the sleeping form of a fat and sweaty businessman. The fat man had his trousers around his ankles and a copy of *Men's Health* magazine spread across his stomach.

'You friggin' arsehole,' he said.

He kicked the fat man in the balls and punched him in the face.

I sighed and took that as my cue to leave. I picked up my bag and went back to the bar.

The barmaid ignored me as I picked up my pint of Guinness. She was filing her nails and staring at the front door.

Drella stood in the doorway. He was looking towards the corner of the room. Staring at the toilet door. He looked angry and more than somewhat psychotic.

The ratty-looking man rushed out of the toilets with a briefcase under his arm. He looked flustered and had stains over his Adidas trainers. He handed the briefcase to Drella and they both left.

I turned to look at the barmaid and maybe ask her what the hell that was all about but now she was stocking a large fridge with garishly coloured alcopops. I concentrated on my drink and was deep in thought when a lanky hipster with a preposterous beard burst out of the toilets, shouting into his iPhone. He called the barmaid over and spoke to her. She looked shocked and dropped the bottle of Bacardi Breezer she'd been holding. It smashed on the floorboards as she ran upstairs. A few minutes later she returned with a red-faced man who was tucking a Seatown United shirt into his jeans. He went into the toilet and came out again looking white, locked the toilet door and went over to the optics. He poured himself a large measure of brandy, drank it down and poured another. The barmaid stood beside him biting her nails.

I was close to the end of my drink when two policemen rushed into the pub. I polished off my pint and slipped out.

I stood on the pavement awash with memories and a sense of dread. I was jolted from my reverie as a woman rode a lime green Vespa past me, splashing me as she drove through a puddle.

'For fuck's sake,' I shouted. 'Watch where you're bloody driving.'

The woman parked up the bike, got off and walked towards me, taking off her helmet. She had short black, spiky hair and a broad grin.

'As I live and breathe, it really is Tommy bloody Bennett. The walking dead himself,' she said.

'Half-dead anyway,' I said.

'You're such a cheeky fucker,' she said. 'Showing your face around here again after all the shit storms you caused back in the day.'

I shrugged. 'Nice to see you too, Tamsin.'

She chuckled and kissed me on the cheek. 'Great to see you, Dad. A real surprise, that's for sure. Are you still on the wagon?' she asked. 'I heard a nasty rumour that you'd taken the pledge when you moved down south.'

'I did for a bit but the wobbly wheels fell off that wagon.'

'Come on then,' she said, dragging me across the rain-soaked street.

'You mean you don't fancy a drink in The Spinal Tap?' I said.

'There's slumming it and there's slumming it,' she said.

'You've got a point. I never thought that place could go down the Swanee but it actually seems to have done so.'

'Let's go in here, it's a bit more civilised.'

We walked into The Park Hotel's pastel-coloured lounge. An old man in a tweed jacket looked up angrily from the *Times* crossword as we came in. Miles Davis played at a low volume. A sleepy dog was curled up near a fruit machine.

'What can I get you?' said Patsy, the pasty-faced

barmaid.

'Gin and tonic for me,' said Tamsin.

'Ice and a slice?' said Patsy.

'Aye.'

Patsy squinted at me. 'Tommy Bennett?' she said.

'The self-same.'

'You've bloody aged, Tommy,' said Patsy. 'I almost didn't recognise you. You look so much like your dad, you know?'

She crossed herself and I shuffled uncomfortably. 'Tamsin takes after her mother, eh?' said Patsy, with a smirk.

'I'll have a pint of Kronenburg, please,' I said.

She shook her head. 'I really and honestly wouldn't have recognised you,' said Patsy, pouring the drinks. 'You used to be so fresh faced.'

'I know, you already said.'

Tamsin collected the drinks. We sat in the corner. A couple of people I recognised from The Seatown Folk Club came in. Patsy said something to them and they looked over. I nodded and they nodded back. I'd been back in Seatown for less than an hour and it was already starting to feel claustrophobic.

My hands were shaking as I sipped my beer. The pub's well-to-do customers were looking at me as if I was something the cat had dragged in. My reputetion still preceded me.

'You just look so much like Grandad now,' said Tamsin, smirking. 'And you've really aged, you know?'

'Well, if I didn't, I do now,' I said.

Tamsin wasn't far from forty but she looked younger. She was dressed all in black apart from a slash of red lipstick and red nail varnish. She was stylish and comfortable with it. I'd had a fling with her mother when I was just out of my teens. Tamsin was born nine months later and her mother and my paths diverged soon after.

'Why are you still in Seatown anyway?' I said. 'You were always raring to get the fuck out of Dodge.'

She finished her drink and crunched the ice cubes. 'You know what John Lennon said about plans.'

'I don't, actually. I always preferred The Rolling Stones.'

Tamsin grinned. It reminded me of the last time I had seen her. She was singing a ropey version of The Banshees' 'Happy House' at the Sixth-Form College karaoke night.

'So, what happened?' I said. 'Or rather, what didn't happen?'

'I got caught up with the minutia of life and let

my big dreams fall to the wayside. Fall and crash. Crash and burn.'

'I know what you mean. Life has a way of wringing your enthusiasms out of you.'

'Very profound, that is.'

'I know. I read it in a book.'

I took another drink.

'Better to be king for a day than a schmuck for a lifetime,' said Tamsin.

'Indeed. Very profound, that.'

'I know, I got it from a film,' she said.

'I know,' I said. 'So what are you up to? Married? Living in sin?'

'Well, I was hitched for a bit but I'm happily divorced now.'

'Were you married to anyone I know?'

'Nick Swinburne. He used to work in the civic centre. Accountant. Remember him?'

'I do. Vaguely,' I said.

I remembered Nick from school. He used to be a bit of an arsehole but I thought it better not to mention it.

'Any kids?' I said.

'A daughter. Nico. She's twenty, would you believe?'

'Time flies. Does she still live in Seatown?'

'No. She's in Leeds studying music.'

'Nice. One that got away, eh?'

Tamsin smiled.

'Aye. One of the lucky ones. Another drink?' she said, tapping my wrist.

'Aye, why not,' I said. 'In for a penny and all that.'

Tamsin went to the bar and I looked out of the window. Seatown had changed more than I'd expected. And for the better by the looks of things. From where I sat, it looked quite nice. But I still wasn't too comfortable to be back.

Tamsin sat back down and put the drinks on the table.

'What brings you back to the frozen wastelands of the north, then?' she said.

'I'm not exactly sure,' I said. 'Nostalgia?'

Tamsin looked sceptical.

'Really?' she said.

'Well, no. I need to lay low for a bit, to be honest.'

'Things hotting up down the big smoke?'

'You could say that.'

'Where are you staying?' she said.

'I might try and rent a bedsit over The Headland.'

'Your mam and auntie Patricia are still here, though, aren't they?'

'Yes and no. Patricia married a southerner, a Jehovah's Witness would you believe. She lives in

Tunbridge Wells. She took the whole brood with her. And Mam's still in that old giff's home near the sea front.'

'How old is she now?'

'Knocking on ninety. Still as batty as a bunch of frogs, I expect.'

'You've not had much contact recently then?' she said.

'Not a lot,' I said. 'You?'

'You know I was never made welcome.'

I frowned and looked out of the window again. Two massive seagulls were fighting over the contents of a rubbish bin. An old man threw a beer can at them but they ignored it.

'I might be able to sort a place out for you. Some friends are off travelling the world and would welcome a house sitter,' said Tamsin.

'Yeah?'

I thought for a minute. It might be a good idea to stay somewhere I had no connection with. Just in case the police—or someone else—came looking for me.

'Yep. I'll send them a text and see when we can pick up the keys,' she said.

She moved next to me and tapped a text out on her phone.

'And do you have any suggestions of what I can

do in the meantime?' I said.

'Well, knock that back and we can go on a bit of a pub crawl,' she said.

'Are there any more decent pubs to crawl to in Seatown?'

'More than enough to meet our needs.'

A thunderstorm ripped the night open and dragged me from my sleep. My swampy brain slowly focused on the silhouette of a large man holding a gun as he stood in front of the bedroom window, the tip of his cigarette glowing and disappearing as he sucked on it. A neon sign flickered outside, lightning flashed and everything turned pitch black. I rubbed my eyes and saw no one was there. I was alone in the room. I closed my eyes and let sleep enfold me.

Tamsin knocked on the bedroom door and woke me up sometime in the early afternoon with a cup of black coffee.

'I didn't put milk or sugar in it,' she said. 'I didn't think you'd be the type.'

'You assumed correctly.'

I sipped the hot coffee and was a little surprised to find that it was instant. Nescafe. Tamsin certainly didn't seem the type. Her house was very rustic. She was a painter and watercolours of local buildings and landmarks adorned the walls. They were good, too.

'How's the coffee?' she said.

She was dressed in a black polo neck sweater and black jeans.

'Great,' I lied.

'Naw, it isn't. It's shit. It's only there for emergencies. I need to do some shopping and buy some proper stuff. I thought we'd go out for breakfast, if you're up for it?'

'Why not. Just give me a few minutes to pull myself around,' I said.

She kissed me on the forehead and headed out of the bedroom.

I put the coffee mug on the bedside table and went into the bathroom for my ablutions. When I came out I saw a fresh set of clothes on the bed.

Tamsin put her head around the door.

'Your clothes were in a bit of a mess after you spilled that kebab over yourself last night so I put them in the wash. I've given you some of my ex-husband's old clobber. It should fit you well enough if you tuck the shirts in.'

'Thanks,' I said, wondering what the hell I'd got myself into.

* * *

'You know, you're a pretty good bullshitter,' said Tamsin. 'Well, when you're sober, that is.'

We were sat in Le Baroque, a suitably trendy coffee bar, having a suitably trendy breakfast. The music was the suitably trendy Nick Drake. It was a new addition to Seatown's culinary repertoire and seemed to be doing quite well.

'What are you insinuating?' I said.

A police car and an ambulance roared past the café. I was starting to feel on edge, the hangover biting a little.

'When you lied about liking the Nescafe I couldn't tell but when you lied last night after a few drinks it was easy to spot because you have a tell,' said Tamsin.

'A what?'

'You know, when poker players bluff some of them have a little habit that gives them away. A little physical tic.'

'And what's mine, pray tell.'

'You pull your right earlobe,' said Tamsin. 'Like Humphrey Bogart in that old film.'

'I do not,' I said, pulling my right earlobe.

'Do too.'

'No way.'

'Yes way,' she said.

Her iPhone buzzed on the table. She picked it up

and read a text message. She smiled.

'Okay, listen up, I have some good news,' she said. 'It looks like you have a place to stay for about a month at least.'

'Tidy,' I said.

'There's no place like home,' she said.

THE FOURTH PART

Of course, I had always felt like one of the eternally discombobulated and never considered anywhere as my home. My family moved around a lot when I was a child—a trend I continued when I grew up. But I still vividly remember the first house I ever lived in, an archetypical, northern, working-class terraced house in Mayfair Road. Two up, two down. Back yard, back street. I was even born on the sofa there. I remember the outside toilet and getting bathed in a metal bath in front of a coal fire. Using old newspapers as toilet paper. The sixties weren't all that swinging in the north of England.

After that, my family moved to similar homes, though they all had bathrooms as far as I could remember. And as an adult, flats above shops were my usual abode of choice. I lived above betting shops, record shops, general dealers and even a wet fish shop—the smell didn't exactly help my many hangovers. I'd lived above a pizza restaurant in

Canning Town and in a swanky apartment block in Chelsea.

But I'd never lived in a place as decidedly hip as Julian and Niki Bogajski's joint. The flat was above a trendy café in Burton Road. And despite the constant racket from the joint below it had cost a packet to buy. Not that Julian and Niki would have known that. He was a photographer and she was a 'food stylist', whatever that was. They spent most of their life traveling around the world taking pictures of food, or something. Hence the Spartan flat.

There were some impressive wildlife photographs on the wall and what I'd been told was a Native American dream catcher hanging over the front door, but furniture was sparse. A sofa and an armchair in the living room. A small bookcase contained a signed collection of Jamie Oliver cookbooks and a half-read copy of *One Hundred Years of Solitude*.

There was an old radiogram and a trendy-looking bed in the bedroom, although the radiogram didn't seem to work. There was, however, an old Sony Walkman and a handful of Peter Gabriel cassettes.

The bathroom was full. Kitted out with what I assumed were top-of-the-range toiletries and cosmetics and a greater variety of towels than I ever thought possible. And none of them stolen from hotels.

The kitchen was surprisingly empty although the stainless-steel fridge was stocked with expensive vodka and cheap champagne, which suited me down to the ground. There were even a couple of cans of Sapporo beer and some Zico coconut water.

I had no idea how long Niki and Julian would be away but was more than happy to house-sit for them. I'd been there a couple of days and was starting to like the place. I could hear the heavy bass of an old Public Image song from somewhere outside as I edged myself off the bed. I was shaking as I went to the kitchen and took a bottle of Stoli Elit vodka from the fridge. I poured a liberal amount into a glass, drank it down in one and peeled back the blinds. The granite sky was filling with black storm clouds. The street was deserted. No people and no ghosts.

I showered, dressed, counted to ten and headed out into the rain to meet my mother.

I had always imagined old people's homes to be depressing. Grey and beige places stinking of piss and disappointment. But Anchor Court was far from that. It was a converted Victorian house in The Headland and the residents' lounge looked out at the sea front. It seemed more like a Butlins for wrinklies, in fact. A couple of people were playing ping pong, there was a Zumba class and the plasma screen television was showing a back-to-back run of Police Academy films.

And my mother was dressed like Shirley Bassey.

'It's Tuesday night, son. Fancy-dress karaoke,' she said.

'What tune are you going to do?' I said.

"Diamonds Are Forever', of course,' she said.

She attempted some sort of hand movement and grimaced. 'Bloody arthritis.'

I looked around the lounge.

'Seems pretty decent here,' I said.

'Not bad at all, Son,' she said.

She leaned forward.

'I'm surprised to see you back here,' she said. 'Bollocks things up down south, did you?'

'Yeah, I did a bit.'

'I've got no dosh you know?'

'I know,' I said.

'Do you ever see the grandkids?'

'Enough. I just don't have the patience for them these days. I've nowt in common with them anyway apart from an accident of birth.'

A man who looked like Barry Manilow announced into the microphone that the karaoke was about to start.

'Best bugger off, Son,' said my mother. 'I don't want you cramping my style.'

So, bugger off I did.

It was a brittle, icy morning and the air tasted like lead. I was still half asleep as I walked along the street but something made me notice the black BMW parked at the end of the street like a shark waiting to attack. I called into a newsagent for a new top-up card for my smartphone and picked up a copy of *Mojo* magazine.

When I came out of the shop, the car was gone. I crossed the road to The Star Coffee Bar, my greasy spoon of choice, and went in.

One of the Dimitriou twins was behind the counter. I nodded to Andy, or maybe it was Jason—I'd never been able to tell the Dimitriou twins apart—and took a seat.

I was feeling a tad maudlin, reflective. I took stock of my situation. I was staying at a friend of a friend's flat but for how long I didn't know. I had no job, no income and my funds were dwindling. I wasn't so much up shit creek without a paddle as without a canoe.

One of the twins brought over a mug of sweet tea.

'Full English, Tommy?' he said.

'I'm not bothered about the scran's nationality as long as it contains meat—and lots of it.'

'Making up for lost time?' he said, referring to my period of vegetarianism.

'For sure. I'm one step from cannibal these days,' I said.

'The things we do for love,' he said.

'Cherchez la femme fatale,' I said.

He chuckled and went behind the counter. He turned up the radio for the midday news, which was followed by a phone-in show about global warming or maybe it was about Brexit and remoaners, whatever they were. It all blurred into one. I opened up *Mojo* and was reading a Roger Waters interview when my fry up was placed unceremoniously on the table. One of the twins changed the radio to an eighties music station and I tucked in.

I'd finished my breakfast and was halfway through my second mug of tea when I saw someone in front of the café. Drella.

He came in and sat in front of me. His face was pallid and his lips were red, as if he'd been scrubbing them with a Brillo pad.

'Morning, Tommy,' he said.

Drella had a raspy voice that only added to the sinister appearance. A Welsh accent lurked below the surface.

'It is that,' I said. 'Unfortunately.'

The wrinkly old waitress brought a black coffee over and put it in front of Drella.

'Thanks Shirley,' he said.

I yawned and rubbed my head.

'Not a morning person, eh?' he said. 'Me neither.'

He sipped the coffee and smiled. 'I tried phoning you a few times but your phone was dead.'

'Yeah, I forgot my charger. Needed to top it up, too,' I said.

'The wife does that all the time. Either that or it's stuffed at the bottom of her handbag and she can't hear it ringing. And don't even mention how often she's lost the house keys.'

'There was a time when you didn't need to lock up your house. Or so they say,' I said.

'Oh, I don't need to lock up my house. It's as safe as...'

'Houses?' I said.

The waitress brought over a bacon sandwich for Drella. The bacon was smothered in brown sauce. He winked at her.

'Ta Shirley. Just the way I like it,' he said.

We sat in silence while he ate. I finished my tea and flicked through the magazine. I realised it was six months old. Someone had drawn moustaches on all the photos of Damon Albarn. I chuckled.

'He's like the Jamie Oliver of the music world,' said Drella.

'Oh, I don't mind old Damon All-bran. Jamie Oliver on the other hand, well, he needs a good smack.'

'I used to love the music mags when I was a nipper,' said Drella. '*Smash Hits. Record Mirror. The Face.* I'm out of the loop now though. Have more pressing concerns.'

'Yeah, it's hard to keep up to date,' I said. 'Slips through your fingers.'

'Yep, it's an elusive fucker is time,' he said.

I was starting to feel edgy.

'Do you still read a newspaper?' he said.

'No so much. I just glance at the BBC headlines on my phone most of the time.'

'Like most of us. So, you probably won't have seen this.'

He took a copy of *The Seatown Mail* from his pocket. 'Have a gander.'

I did.

The front page was a story about a body that had been found in The Tap and Spile's toilets.

'For fuck's sake,' I muttered.

'Yep, indeed,' said Drella.

Drella got up. 'Let's go for a proper drink. We

need to talk,' he said.

'Yeah?'

'Yeah.'

I stood up and took out my wallet. 'I need to pay my bill.'

'No you don't,' he said. 'It's on the house.'

'Know the owner, do you?'

'I am the owner.'

He waved to the waitress, who blew him a kiss, and we left.

'It's got a hell of a history this place, you know? They even say you used to be able to hire a contract killer back in fifties,' said Drella. 'Not just some daft rent-a-thug, either. A full-on hit man. It doesn't seem likely now.'

We were sat in The Cobble Bar, a pub just off the high street. The place wasn't actually open for a few more hours but it didn't seem to stop Drella from getting a couple of pints of John Smith's Smooth and a plate of chicken curry. I couldn't face food. I was having trouble keeping down my breakfast after what I'd read in the newspaper. The dead man's identity had been a bit of a shocker and then some. I'd come back to Seatown to escape...that sort of thing. Maybe it just wasn't possible.

'I suppose Seatown has a bit of a chequered history,' I said.

'Most of us have a bit of chequered history, Tommy. You, for example. I've been nosing around with my contacts down the soft south. You've been up to all sorts of shenanigans since you left Seatown. Shacking up with a gangster's moll in Canning Town? Risky, that. And if what they tell me about your jobs for Jeffrey Munday is true, well...'

He leaned across the table. 'You are not what you appear to be are you, Tommy? You've pulled off a few phenomenal jobs over the years and yet you've never spent as much as a day behind bars. Quite impressive really.'

'Well, I...'

He waved a hand.

'Don't worry Tommy,' said Drella. 'I'm not that interested in what you've done. Not fussed. It's like Morrissey said, all men have secrets, and I'm certainly not going to share mine.'

'So why are we here?' I said.

'Now there's a big question. Philosophers have pondered that for aeons, for donkey's years. But as for me and you, well, I'm here to offer you a job.'

'Yeah?'

'Yep. No heavy stuff but a tad on the dodgy side.'

I thought about my dwindling funds and smiled.

'So, how can I be of service?' I said.

'I'll get another round in and then I'll tell you.'

Drella went over to the bar. I knocked back the dregs of my pint. My eyes were sore. I took out my contact lenses and put my glasses on.

'Now, that's not what I expect a successful hit man to look like,' said Drella, putting the drinks on the table. 'Not that we should judge by appearances, eh? I mean people might look at me and think I'm a dangerous gangster. A psychopath.'

He leaned close.

'And I am,' he said.

He chuckled and I noticed he was staring over my shoulder. I turned and saw a twitchy, ratty-looking man leaning against the bar watching us. The same one I'd seen in The Tap and Spile when I'd first got back to Seatown.

'Is that a friend of yours?' I said.

'He's more of a business acquaintance,' said Drella. 'I don't think Sniffy is the friend type.'

He nodded and the man came over.

'Tommy, this is Sniffy,' said Drella.

'Pleasure,' said Sniffy. He sniffed.

I nodded. 'I'm Tommy.'

'I know,' said Sniffy.

'Okay,' said Drella. 'Enough of the sparkling

repartee. Drink up. We've work to do.'

He stood and loomed over me. I knocked back my drink. I was about to take a leap into the mire and hoped it would all come out in the wash.

'You see the difference between Bruce Willis's smirk and Ryan Gosling's is that Willis looks like he's smirking to himself, looking at himself in the mirror. Lapping it up. But Gosling looks like he's had a funny turn and he stayed like that. Know warra mean, like?' said Sniffy.

'I do,' I said. Though I didn't.

We were sat in the back of Drella's BMW. Drella was driving. Slowly. It was almost midnight and the streetlights flickered as we headed to the edge of town. Lee Perry's 'Super Ape' played at a low volume. Sniffy was dressed in what he described as his Sunday best: a black pinstripe suit and black shirt with a white tie. His hair was slicked back. He'd snorted an impressive amount of Colombian sprinting powder earlier and was inevitably talking ten to the dozen. I kept catching Drella's reflection in the mirror and it looked as if he was enjoying the scenario. His big rictus grin made him look like the Joker.

The music changed to The Upsetters' 'The Return

of Django' as we pulled into the car park of a closed down nightclub. The Rialto. The car park was covered with shards of broken glass that glittered like stars.

Sniffy chuntered on but I'd managed to tune him out.

'What's the plan, then?' I said.

'We listen to the music,' said Drella.

The next song was Barrington Levy's 'Murder'. Drella turned and looked at me.

'This is your theme song,' he said.

He grinned.

'Arf,' I said.

Rivulets of rain ponderously trailed down the windscreen. When the music finished, Drella switched off the engine.

'Let's go to work,' he said. 'You bugger off first, Sniffy.'

Sniffy sniffed and got out of the car. I saw he was wearing a shoulder strap under his jacket. He walked towards the closed-down club. As he opened the metal door, a blast of hard rock burst free. It sounded like Black Sabbath. A truck pulled into the car park and a skinhead in a tartan shirt got out and went into the pub. I felt frozen. Trapped like one of the wasps I used to catch in jam jars when I was a kid.

Drella's phone buzzed and he checked a text message.

'Off we jolly well go,' he said.

We got out of the car and Drella opened up the boot. He took out a black Adidas holdall and handed it to me.

We walked across the car park.

'I didn't even know this place was still open,' I said.

'It isn't,' said Drella.

He opened the door and we stepped into the darkness. My senses were overwhelmed. Dope, cigarettes, sweat and some smells I didn't want to think about. Black Sabbath's 'War Pigs' melded with laughter and screams. When my eyes adjusted I saw the place was full. The only lighting was red lamps placed around the room.

'Follow me,' said Drella.

We went into another room. The skinhead I'd seen earlier stood at a long bar talking to Sniffy. The barmaid was a tall transvestite I remembered was called Ava Banana. She used to have a very successful musical act back in the day. We went over to the bar and I could see the skinhead was already tiring of Sniffy's conversation.

Drella tapped Sniffy on the shoulder.

'Come on,' he said.

We followed Drella through a red cushioned door and it was as if we'd stepped into another world rather than another room.

'Welcome to Narnia,' said Drella.

The smell was different. Perfume and flowers. There even appeared to be a segregated smoking section. The music was Frank Sinatra's 'Watertown' and the décor was like a fifties New York jazz bar.

'Class,' I said.

'Like something from a dream, eh?' said Drella.

I followed him over to a small, red booth. We sat down and within seconds a tiny waiter in a red waistcoat limped over to us.

'What can I get you gents?' he said.

'Three pints of lager for us and whatever Bev's having,' said Drella.

The waiter nodded and limped away.

'Bev?' I said. 'Bev Ferry, I assume.'

'Aye. Bev Ferry,' said Drella. 'I think you know each other.'

'Oh, aye,' I said. 'We went to school together.'

'You know her better than that, I think. Didn't you used to go out with her?' said Drella.

He glared at Sniffy, who was grinding his teeth.

'Yeah. Back in the day. I knew the whole family.'

'I imagine that brother of hers was a bit of a handful, eh?' said Drella.

'Most of the time he was fine. I mean, I like Craig. We've known each other for donkey's years. But when he was snorting the happy talc he could be a right pain in the arse.'

'Yes, it makes reasonable people into arseholes that stuff,' said Drella. 'And if they're already arseholes, well...'

He nodded at Sniffy.

'What do you think, Sniffy?' said Drella.

'Eh, I'll tell you. I'll tell you who I really hate. Who I just cannot fucking stand,' said Sniffy. He sniffed again.

'Who's that, then?' I said.

I hadn't known him that long but I'd known Sniffy long enough to know the list of people he loathed was damned near endless.

'Angie friggin' Bowie', said Sniffy. 'I saw her on that *Celebrity Big Brother* when David croaked. What a cow. I mean, first of all she takes her ex-husband's name—and it's not even his real name it's his stage name! Her first ex-husband at that! She didn't call herself Angie Blood after her other husband. I wonder why not? What a slapper. And now she thinks she wrote all of his songs because she told David what jumper to wear in 1972!'

'Who was her other husband, then? I can't remember him,' I said.

'A bloke called Drew Blood. He was in some failed punk band or other.'

'Yeah? Can't say I've heard of him.'

'He was an American, I think,' said Sniffy.

'Oh, well. That'll be why, then,' I said.

The waiter brought the drinks and as he went away Bev Ferry came over.

'Grab us me chair please, Gimp,' she said.

Bev smiled but there was the familiar razor-sharp look in her eyes. She was dressed in white, with white lipstick and eye makeup. Her hair was naturally raven black but she'd dyed it blonde.

'Nice to see you back home, Tommy. Last time I saw you, you left with a hell of a bang,' she said.

I cringed.

She grinned.

Gimp and a big red-haired biker brought over a white leather armchair and Bev sat down. Drella passed the Adidas bag over to her. She nodded and picked up her drink.

'Ta much,' she said.

'You're welcome,' said Drella.

'Chin chin,' she said.

'Cheers,' said Drella.

'Up your Khyber!' said Sniffy.

He chuckled but everyone else just glared at him. He sniffed loudly.

'I've got my boogie boots on!' he said.

He got up and went over to a small deserted dancefloor. He started cutting shapes like he was dancing to acid house and not Sinatra. Drella put his head in his hands.

'He must have come close to death more times than he realises, that bloke,' said Bev.

'Probably, but I reckon Sniffy's a survivor,' said Drella. 'Like our friend Tommy here.'

'Cheers,' I said.

'Which brings us down to business,' said Bev.

'Tell me more, tell me more. I'm all Mick Hucknall,' I said.

'I'll get us another round and we can talk,' said Bev.

She held up a hand and clicked her fingers three times like a Flamenco dancer. Gimp was over with a fresh round of drinks within seconds.

'The thing is,' said Drella. 'Bev and I have a little business deal going on at the moment and we need a Harry Lime.'

'Sorry?' I said.

'A third man,' said Bev.

I looked towards Sniffy who was now pogoing to 'Fly Me to the Moon'.

'I thought you already had one,' I said.

'Him?' said Bev. 'Not a chance. He's a perennial

fuck up. A disaster waiting to happen. We need someone with more than two brain cells to rub together. Anyway, Sniffy's a cokehead. You can only tell him so much, he's such a blabbermouth. The world and its mother-in-law would know what we're up to sooner than you can say Jack Robinson.'

'So, what's the story, morning glory?' I said.

'I'm sure you remember the corpulent gentleman that you saw dead in the toilets at The Spinal Tap?' said Drella.

'I do,' I said. 'It wasn't a pretty sight.'

'I'm sure. And as you now know he died of a heart attack because of an overdose of cocaine and Viagra.'

'I'm sure Sniffy giving him a good kicking didn't help a great deal,' I said.

'Oh, he was already dead by then. Anyway, you also now know that the bloke's name was Nick Swanbourne. Erstwhile husband of your daughter Tamsin,' said Drella.

Bev winked at me. Blew a kiss.

'Yeah. He was an accountant at the civic centre, I think,' I said.

'Not just any accountant. Nick was the chief accountant. He had a lot control over Seatown local government's finances and was very useful as far as money laundering is concerned.'

'I see. But what I don't see is how I can help. I'm no accountant. I need a calculator to work out how old I am.'

'Yes,' said Bev, leaning close to me. 'But we don't need an accountant. We need a man.'

'A man of the cloth, to be precise,' said Drella.

Bev grinned and Drella started laughing. He pushed a hand into his jacket pocket and took out a priest's dog collar.

'What do you think, Father Tommy? Are you game?' said Drella.

I crossed myself. 'Spectacles, testicles, wallet and watch.'

There was a bang and the skinhead truck driver I'd seen earlier burst into the room wielding a hammer. His nose was bleeding and his eyes were just as red.

'Thieving fucker,' he said and ran towards the stage where Sniffy was dancing the Macarena to an Ella Fitzgerald song.

As he rushed past us, Bev stood and wrapped an arm around the skinhead's neck. She twisted, tripped him and he fell to the ground yelling.

Bev stretched and sat back down as Gimp and another man dragged the skinhead into a store room. Gimp took a baseball bat from behind the bar.

'I though this room was invitation only,' said Drella.

'Yeah, we really need to get a proper lock on that door,' said Bev.

She turned towards the dancefloor.

'Leave Sniffy here when you go,' she said. 'I need to have a word with him about selling dodgy shit on my premises.'

I saw Gimp cleaning blood from the baseball bat and didn't fancy Sniffy's chances.

'So, what's with the priest gig, then?' I said. 'You know I'm not even a Catholic.'

'It should be a piece of piss,' said Bev.

Gimp brought a tray of vodka shots over. I was starting to feel drunk.

'Do you remember Father Malloy?' said Bev.

'I remember seeing him hanging around the amusement arcades on the sea front,' I said. 'And near the sea cadets' hall.'

'Yes, he did have some distasteful...habits,' said Bev. 'But he served his purposes from time to time. The trouble is, he's recently gone missing. And we're of need of his services.'

'So, you want me to impersonate a priest?' I said.

'Got it in one,' said Drella. 'Before he croaked, Nick Swinburne told us that one of the councillors—a bloke called Pike—was thinking about blabbing to the law about our dubious business enterprises. Turns out the bloke's a rampant Catholic and he's had a crisis of conscience and wants to come clean. And we want you to persuade him otherwise.'

'Is it the same Pike that used to be a teacher at my school?' I said.

'It is,' said Bev.

'And if he doesn't agree?' I said.

'Sic transit Gloria bloody Gaynor,' said Drella.

THE FIFTH PART

I was falling asleep as we drove in silence down the coastal road. The roadside was cluttered with billboards. Adverts for fast food joints, nightclubs and casinos.

'Who can afford to go to casinos around here?' I said. 'I thought Seatown was still an unemployment hotspot?'

'It is indeed,' said Drella. 'But since the new motorway opened up from Seatown to Newcastle, the town has started to get awash with coachloads of pissed up Geordies.'

'Sounds delightful,' I said.

The sun was creeping over the horizon. The sky was melting from black to grey. I noticed a familiar face on one of the billboards. There was an election coming up in Seatown and the billboard showed the grinning profile of one of the prospective candidates. It seemed that Councillor Pike was a candidate for The Great Britain Independence Party.

I saw a pack of bikers riding across the beach wearing wolf masks. A couple of skinheads were feeding sweetcorn and bicarbonate of soda to the seagulls. When the birds flew down to drink some seawater they exploded mid-air. It had been the height of hilarity when I was a kid.

'There were rumours at my school that Pike was a bit of a nonce, if I remember correctly,' I said.

'He'll fit in well at GBIP then,' said Drella. 'They're a right bunch of weirdos and oddballs.'

'Politics, that great cesspool into which the flotsam and jetsam of life are inevitably drawn,' I said.

'Indeed,' said Drella.

'I was thinking about Jack Martin earlier tonight. He ran this town like the German railway back in the day. You worked for him for a bit, didn't you?'

'Aye. He was a hard bastard, was Jack. Remember that thing he used to say, about how ninety per cent of Seatown's population were just here to make up the numbers.'

'Cannon fodder. Shit people living shit lives shitting out more shit people,' I said.

'He may have hated Seatown but he never left the bloody place, though,' said Drella.

'Yeah, he's still here now in The West Park Cemetery,' I said.

We were both laughing as Drella pulled up outside my flat.

'Right. Get some kip and take it easy on the booze,' he said. 'We've got a big day tomorrow night.'

I yawned and opened the door.

'What do you think will happen to Sniffy?' I said.

'Oh, he'll be alright. Like I said, he's got the survivor's gene. If he fell in the North Sea he'd come out with a pocket full of fish.'

He looked at his Rolex watch.

'Oh, bugger,' he said. 'I'd best get a move on. The missus wants me to take her to IKEA today and if I'm late she'll have my guts for garters.'

The heavy autumn rain battered The Cobble Bar's arch-shaped windows like bullets from a machine gun. As I crossed the road, a man in a long, black coat rushed past the pub holding a black umbrella that flapped in the wind like a bat's wings. I walked through the double doors and into the darkened bar.

Inside, multi-coloured lanterns adorned the room and the pub's few tables were lit up by large candles that had melted into strangely shaped wax sculptures. Apart from the bar area, which twinkled and sparkled, the rest of the pub was in pitch black darkness.

Franny, the Scouse barman, sat on a stool at the end of the bar reading a torn old copy of the seventies music magazine *Sounds*. The stained cover featured a photograph of The Teardrop Explodes. He occasionally ran a hand through his big ginger quiff, leaving ink stains on his forehead. He sipped from a bottle of Fanta, sometimes nodding. He was wearing a black Gene Vincent t-shirt, shorts and trainers. The pub was stiflingly hot.

A sweaty, middle-aged man in a black leather jacket was pumping a ton of coins into the Wurlitzer jukebox. The Saints' 'I'm Stranded' finished and Lou Reed started singing about a 'Satellite of Love'. The man started to sing along.

I leaned against the bar. The sleeve of my jacket plonked in a pool of spilt snakebite. I wrung it dry and sat on a barstool.

'Evening. What can I get you tonight Tommy?' said Franny.

'A pint of Guinness and a Jack Daniels would do very nicely indeed,' I said.

'Double or single Jack?'

'Aw, make it a double. Better to be hung for a sheep than a lamb.'

I took off my jacket and put it on the stool next to mine. I peeled off the price tag from the tartan Ben Sherman shirt I'd bought from the Scope shop. The shirt still smelled second-hand despite the aftershave I'd soaked myself with.

'Hot in here, eh?' said Franny as he put the whiskey in front of me.

'A bit, yeah,' I said.

I paid for my drink.

'The heating's knackered. It's either too hot or too cold,' said Franny. 'But the owner's too tight to pay and get it fixed.'

'Can't you open a window or two?' I said.

Franny grinned. 'Around here? You must be joking,' he said. 'They're locked shut. Health and safety rules or not.'

'I'll just have to cope, then,' I said.

I contemplated my glass of Jack Daniels. The ice cubes shimmered in the wan light. The effects of the previous night's drinking session were still washing over me.

The Cobble Bar was a like a time machine. A warm womb protecting its middle-aged habitués from the harsh light of the twenty-first century. No Wi-Fi. No television, and mobile phones were banned. I loved it there.

Outside, the wet pavement reflected the bar's flickering neon sign. As Lou Reed segued into The Doors, Sniffy burst through the door, growling. I could tell Sniffy wasn't a happy man, even by his usual morose standards. His black raincoat was soaked and he held a broken, black umbrella limply in his bandaged hand. His long black hair hung like rats' tails.

Sniffy, as twitchy and sweaty as usual, stumbled towards the bar, grunting at Franny. His red eyes glared at all and sundry. Franny poured Sniffy's pint of John Smith's Smooth and quickly tried to slip the music magazine out of Sniffy's sight but wasn't fast enough.

'Copey? Julian fuckin Cope? That tosser ripped off his whole fuckin act from the likes of Mark E. Smith and Ian Curtis,' said Sniffy, his arms waving wildly like a deranged mime artist.

Sniffy struggled to lift his pint glass since the fingers of both hands had recently been broken so he leaned over and sipped it.

'Shall I get you a straw?' said Franny who had a wide grin on his face.

'Actually that's not a bad idea,' said Sniffy.

Franny took a shoe box from under the bar and rummaged in it. 'There you go,' he said.

He took out a plastic bag filled with straws and handed it to Sniffy who looked at it with contempt.

'How am I supposed to open that, like?' he said.

Franny sighed and opened it. He put a couple of straws in Sniffy's pint glass. '*Na zdrowia!*' said Franny.

'What's that when it's at home?' said Sniffy.

'It's Polish for cheers,' said Franny.

'Well, aren't we the cunnilingual one,' said Sniffy. 'Friggin' Scouser can't even speak English.'

He turned to me and wiped the residue of cocaine from his nose.

'Do you remember that lot?' said Sniffy tapping the music paper.

'Of course I do,' I said, yawning. 'Good band, Teardrop Explodes. Better than the Bunnymen for my money.'

'I agree. And I do remember that lot. The Liverpool lot. Scousers like what you are, Franny.'

He jabbed a bandaged finger towards Franny and turned back to me.

'There were three of them, you know what I'm talking about?'

I did know but I also knew it was a waste of time trying to interrupt Sniffy during one of his rants.

'Yeah, there were three of them. Full of themselves, they were. They even called themselves The Crucial Three, for fuck's sake. There was Pete Wylie, he was a good lad, mind you. And Mac. He was alright except for the daft hairstyle. And then there was that tosser Copey, their boring, soppy middle-class friend. He was like a hanger on. A Billy No-Mates.'

'Julian Cope's not actually a Scouser. He's Welsh,' said Franny.

Sniffy snorted. 'That's even worse, then. Anyway, one minute he's hovering around kissing everyone in Liverpool and Manchester's arse and the next thing you know he's on The Old Grey Whistle Test dropping acid, done up in fancy dress and trying to convince everyone he's interesting, weird. An English friggin' eccentric. He's about as eccentric as Nicholas friggin' Parsons. He was a maths teacher or some-thing. What a fucking fake. And another thing, if he hadn't...'

I zoned out and waited for Sniffy to burn himself out with his ranting. I focused on the music. It was Iggy Pop now. By the end of 'Lust For Life', well into his second pint, Sniffy was almost sanguine.

Sniffy drained his drink. I finished mine.

'Another?' said Franny.

'Why not?' I said. 'I could be dead tomorrow.'

I went to the toilet for a tinkle and returned to the sound of Sniffy's raucous laughter.

'Grown men eating breakfast cereals, playing computer games and watching *Star Wars* friggin' films. I mean, that's why the world's gone to friggin' pot. The so-called men are just adult babies. Jelly babies,' said Sniffy.

He pushed away the massive fantasy novel that he'd caught Franny reading and had inspired his latest rant. It crashed onto the dirty floorboards.

I laughed and picked up Franny's book. I dusted it off and handed it to Franny.

'Ta,' he said.

Sniffy snorted.

'Is it any good?' I said.

Franny's eyes lit up. 'Yeah. It's part of a trilogy about a planet of talking—'

I held up a hand.

'I'm only being polite, son,' I said. 'I don't really want to know. It's not my kind of book. My balls have dropped, you know.'

Sniffy started cackling.

I sipped my warm, flat drink. I suddenly felt devoid of sparkle.

'Mind you, kids these days are all wimps too what with their allergies and ADHD and dyslexia and that,' said Sniffy. 'I'll tell you the best way to cure dyslexia is to slap them on the back of the head so the letters all fall into place. Works for that not paying attention thing as well.'

'What does DNA stand for?' said Franny.

'National Dyslexic Association,' I said.

'You've heard it before, then?' said Franny.

'Of course, he has, son. It's as old as the hills,' said Sniffy.

The front door creaked and Drella came in looking worn.

'Sartre got it wrong, I tell you,' he said. 'Hell is IKEA.'

'Fun afternoon?' I said.

'I'd rather have my prostate examined,' said Drella.

'Me too!' said Sniffy.

He cackled and sniffed.

'What's the score with my fancy dress party?' I said.

'You're on tonight,' said Drella. 'Councillor Pike will attend confession at St Martin's church at midnight. You can grab him there.'

'Fair enough. It was a long time ago but there's a chance he might recognise me from school,' I said.

'Just keep your confession box dark,' said Drella.

'And turn your collar up,' said Sniffy.

At seven minutes to midnight, I walked up the gravel path towards St Martin's church. I wore Sniffy's long leather coat over my black suit. I was stone cold sober though I did have a hip flask of rum in my jacket pocket in case of emergency. I wore a pair of wraparound shades and found it hard to see.

The church door was open and I went inside. It was dimly lit and cold. I shuffled into the confession box and sat. I took a sip of rum and waited. The door to the confessional opened.

'Father I need to confess something,' said Pike.

'Mortal or venal,' I said. I tried to change my voice but it sounded like I had laryngitis.

'Venal, I think,' said Pike.

'Go on, my son,' I said, sounding like a northern Frank Butcher.

'Bless me Father, for I have sinned,' said Pike. 'It's been five weeks since my last confession.'

'Go on,' I said, leaning my head against the lattice grid and closing my eyes.

Pike prattled on for ages about the various dodgy activities he was involved in, not just with Bev Ferry and Drella, and it was more than somewhat illuminating. Seatown really was a smorgasbord of crime.

'And what are your intentions, my son,' I rasped.

'Father, I've come to realise that the only way to ease my conscience is if I tell the police about my crimes. To confess. To come clean and take my punishment,' he said.

'But don't you fear violent retribution from these

criminal associates of yours?'

'They can only punish me in this life. The damnation of my immortal soul is in the hands of…'

I drifted off. I'd been trying to think of a way to keep him shtum and decided to give it a shot.

'But what if the police find out about Janice Warren,' I said. 'And Lynne Stalley. And Roberta Cowin.'

I heard Pike gasp. 'How? How could you…?' he said.

'The good lord knows all,' I said. 'And he is most displeased.'

'But…I was just…'

'And then there was Penny Case and Cherry Stone and…'

I heard a bump and more gasping. Then nothing.

'My son,' I said. 'Are you alright?'

Silence.

'Mr Pike?' I said.

Still silence.

'Are you okay?' I said.

I waited a few moments and went into the confessional

Pike was collapsed on the floor in a heap. I turned him over and checked his breathing and his pulse. He was as dead as Di and Dodi.

I chuckled and took out my smartphone. I sent a

text message to Drella: Come to church. Problem solved. Divine intervention.

The Rialto was full though Sniffy was noticeable by his absence as he was still barred.

'It was a good idea naming all those lasses Pike was supposed to have fiddled with,' said Drella. 'A moment of inspiration.'

'It was hard to remember the girls' names, mind you. I hadn't thought about them for years. They were easily forgettable.'

'Not so forgettable for Pike though, eh?' he said.

'It seems that way. Has he been...relocated?'

'Oh, yes, I'd advise you not to buy any bacon from the organic butcher's shop on Merry Street for a few weeks.'

I gulped. 'Thanks. I'd been thinking of going veggie again anyway. Sort of clinches it, that does.'

Gimp brought a bucket of champagne over.

'On the house,' said Gimp.

'Very nice,' said Drella.

'And what exactly are we celebrating?' I said.

'Bev Ferry's recent nomination as Mayor of Seatown,' said Gimp.

'What a tangled web,' I said.

'There's always more going on than you see on

the surface in Seatown,' said Drella.

I noticed Bev was stood with a couple of local councillors and Vince Sandal, an ex-copper who was so bent you could use him to unblock your toilet. They were looking my way.

'It looks as if the local elite are showing an interest in you,' said Drella. 'How are your funny handshaking skills?'

I stuck two fingers up at him. He laughed.

Bev waved to me and gestured me over and I knew that very soon I could be so deep in the Seatown mire you'd need an excavator to get me out. I thought about pretending I hadn't seen her but eventually I stood up and went over. That champagne had tasted pretty nice, after all.

THE SIXTH PART

The office was all shiny chrome and red and black leather. Like something out of *Miami Vice*. It was a look that had been very popular in Seatown once upon a time, especially for men of an uncertain age. Vince Sandal had even gone for the Don Johnson look himself but all the fake tan, paisley suits and expensive cologne couldn't hide that Sandal was an overweight ex-copper in his seventies, complete with the prerequisite boozer's nose and smoker's cough. I wondered if he and Bernie Clarke had the same tailor.

I sipped my cappuccino. I'd decided to stay off the booze for a few days to get my head around some sort of plan to help me escape from Seatown's noose. My ever-decreasing cash had helped with that decision. After disposing of Bernie and Scarecrow, I hadn't wanted to take a chance on going back to my flat in London so I headed straight to Seatown. Without a passport, there weren't too many places I could travel to and I'd need to get some cash together to get a new fake one.

Sandal stood looking out of the office window, smoking a cigar and drinking brandy from a glass so big it should have had a goldfish in it.

'Great view, eh?' he said.

'Tidy,' I said.

Outside his office window was the old disused Seatown Fun Palace. The fun fair had been a local success but European Union health and safety rules forced it to be closed down years before. Sandal, however, had a plan to reanimate it.

'You see a lot people in this town hate the European Union. What with the bombardment and all that's quite understandable. The Germans did a lot of bloody damage to Seatown over the years. But the past is dead and gone. You've got to get with it. Get with the times,' said Sandal. 'You've got to adapt if you want to avoid becoming a dinosaur.'

'So what's your plan?' I said.

I shuffled in my seat. The leather chair creaked.

'Zombies,' he said.

'Zombies?'

'Yes, Zombies. They're all the rage these days. *The Walking Dead, Resident Evil*. Computer games, films and the like. They're as daft as a brush of course but some people love them and not just bairns either. Even grown men. So, my plan is to open up a Zombieland where stag parties and office dos can come and chase zombies around the fairground, like.'

'Where are you going to get the zombies from?' I said.

'Oh, that won't be a problem. I'll get a few community service urchins to do it. Max from Max Magic Shop said he'll get the make-up and clobber sorted out then Bob's your uncle and Fanny's your aunt. What do you think?'

'You know, it's actually a pretty good idea. But what do you want me for?'

'I want you to have a word with someone. To use your powers of persuasion, like. See, although I own The Fun Palace—I bought it for a song from Babs Hammonds few years back—I don't own all of it. There's someone who owns five per cent and I don't want him getting a piece of my potentially lucrative pie. So, if you can track him down, I can make him an offer for their five per cent and all will be hunky dory. Nowt dodgy, like. Well, not unless you have to.'

'Sounds fair enough. Who is it you want me to find?' I said.

'He's an old schoolmate of yours, actually. Bryn Collinson. Think you'll be able to locate him?'

'Shouldn't exactly be a stretch,' I said.

* * *

My stomach rumbled as I walked along the almost deserted coast road. I crossed the road towards the Cod Almighty fish and chip shop and noticed a spruced up E Type Jag parked outside. Sat in the driving seat was an equally spruced up Bryn Collinson, AKA Bryn Lahden.

Once upon a time Bryn had been the archetypal sleazy hack. A dishevelled, boozy, chain-smoking journo in Oxfam suits. On one of my rare visits to Facebook I saw he had cleaned up his act big time. And, indeed, he looked like a Mormon.

He stuck his head out of the car window.

'Tommy bloody Bennett as I live and breathe,' he said. 'The rumours were true then. You've returned to the womb of your home town.'

'A womb with a view,' I said.

I looked towards the closed down Chunky Chicken Factory, which was slap bang in the middle of a couple of rundown amusement arcades.

'Yes, Seatown's as quaint and picturesque a place as ever,' said Bryn.

'You're looking pretty slick. Won the lottery?' I said.

'Not far from it. Uncle Quentin finally snuffed.'

A green Vespa raced by and beeped its horn. I

waved.

'Really? I thought that old rascal would have lived forever,' I said.

'Me too but it turned out he drowned in the bath after drinking some hookey Russian vodka.'

Bryn chuckled.

'It's the way he would have liked to have gone, I think,' I said.

'True enough,' said Bryn. 'Anyway, he left everything he had to me.'

'I never knew he had anything to leave. He'd been on invalidity benefit as long as I could remember.'

'I thought the same but it turned out he'd had his fingers in more than a few pies. He had shares in properties all over the place.'

'Including the Fun Palace?'

'Indeed.'

'Nice one,' I said. 'Fancy a pint?'

'Naw, I'm all health and fitness and safety these days. Except for the odd bag of chips, like.'

He nodded towards the fish and chip shop.

'Come on then,' I said. 'You're buying, of course.'

'Wouldn't have it any other way,' said Bryn.

As we walked in, a busker across the road started singing 'The Times They Are Changing'.

I sat at a gleaming white Formica table while

Bryn ordered the food. A few minutes later he put a tray down on the table.

'That's for you,' he said, pointing to a plate of cod, chips and mushy peas.

'Look's great,' I said.

'It is. But I'll stick with the chips. Trying to keep the weight down, you know?'

'Sort of,' I said.

We tucked in and ate in silence for a few moments. The food was as good as I'd hoped.

'Have you got any work on?' said Bryn.

'Bits and bobs. I've just got a finder's job.'

'For anyone I know?'

'I couldn't possibly breach client confidentiality.'

'Oh, aye. So who is it, then?' he said.

I told him.

He laughed.

'So that's why you asked to meet,' he said. 'I thought you'd missed me.'

'I was going to call, like.'

Bryn wiped his hands on a napkin and took out his smartphone. He tapped on the screen and showed it to me.

'Read that email,' he said.

I did. I whistled.

'That's a tidy offer,' I said. 'I doubt Vince Sandal would be able to match it.'

'I might be willing to offer him a staff discount, like.'

'Really? And not for sentimental reasons, I assume.'

'I'm in need of Sandal's connections in the force. If he scratches my back, well, you know the score.'

'Itchy are you?' I said.

'Very.'

'I'll have a word, then.'

'You know, there's a thin line between being able to multi-task and ADHD,' I said.

We were walking alongside the pond in West Park. Bryn was attempting to send a text message and feed the ducks at the same time. He'd almost thrown the phone into the water.

'Yeah,' he grunted. 'Funny.'

A fat man in a grubby blue bunny rabbit costume walked past. He stuffed a pork pie into his mouth and took a swig from a can of Tango. A few ducks followed his trail of crumbs.

There was a shout and we turned to see a red-faced man in a uniform running towards us waving a clipboard.

'Can you read?' he wheezed. 'Can you read bloody English?'

He pointed to a fading DON'T FEED THE DUCKS sign that some wag had defaced to say DON'T FEED THE FUCKS.

'Ah, that,' I said. 'It isn't that clear, is it?'

'I'll be reporting you to the RSPCA,' said the park keeper. He took out his smartphone.

'Oh, bugger this for a game of soldiers,' said Bryn.

He grabbed the man's phone and threw it in the pond.

'Hey, you can't do that,' said the keeper. 'That's private property. I'll have you arrested. I'll...'

Then Bryn pushed the park keeper into the water and poured bread crumbs over him.

'Let's piss off,' I said as the flapping ducks pecked at the screaming park keeper. 'I'm not at two with nature.'

Bryn burped. He'd perked up about half way through his second can of Fanta and had just polished off a plate of cheeseburger and chips. He'd clearly ditched his diet, if not the sobriety pledge.

He stretched and yawned.

'You still not heard from Sandal?' he said.

'Maybe. My battery died about half an hour ago. I don't suppose you have a Samsung charger on you?' I said.

'Not as such. But they might have one behind the bar. I'll ask.'

I looked around The Red Admiral which was, in fact, unrelentingly beige. Not just the decor but also the customers. Flecks of dust floated in the wan light. A couple of old men silently played chess. Dire Straits played at a low volume. I was drifting off to sleep when Bryn sat back down with two pints of alcohol-free beer in his hands and a Samsung battery charger draped around his neck. He put down the pints and handed me the charger.

'There you go,' he said.

I looked around for a wall socket and found one near a broken-down Space Invaders machine. I plugged it in and sat back down.

'You know, there are plenty of ways to get out of Seatown. You don't need a wad of money,' said Bryn.

'Name one,' I said.

'You get a job.'

He chuckled.

'A proper job? Yeah, that would be right. I might as well stay here if I'm going to go back to soul-sapping drudgery.'

'You could go abroad. Open up an ex-pats bar in Spain, or something.'

'Yeah, but I'd still need some walking around

money to get me a new passport and to get me started,' I said. 'Unless you want to lend me some.'

'Er, no.'

'Thought not.'

'How much is Vince Sandal going to pay you?' he said.

'Not enough, I'm sure,' I said. 'Speaking of which.'

I went over and checked my phone. There was a text message from Sandal. I read it and went back to Bryn.

'Sandal says yes,' I said.

'Tidy,' said Bryn. 'Did he say when we can meet to sort stuff out?'

'He wants you to phone him tomorrow.'

'Great,' said Bryn. 'Everything's coming up roses.'

'Aye. Shit's good for roses.'

I woke up on Tamsin's sofa. The early morning sun was slipping through a gap in the curtains, picking out specks of dust. The television was still switched on from the night before. It was showing an episode of *NCIS*. David McCallum was looking in pretty good nick for his age.

'I have some good news and some bad news,' said Tamsin, as she handed me a can of Irn Bru.

'What's the bad news?' I said.

'Niki and Julian are coming back to Seatown next week. You'll have to move out of their flat.'

I sighed.

'And the good news?' I said.

'You could move in with me? This is a big and empty house I've got. Nico hardly ever comes back. What do you think?'

'I'm not sure, to be honest,' I said. 'I wasn't planning on hanging around Seatown, as you know.'

She sat next to me.

'Have a think about it,' she said. 'I was at the solicitor's yesterday sorting out Nick's last will and testament. While I was waiting, Bev Ferry came in and we had a little natter.'

'Oh yes. Hubble, bubble, toil and trouble, was it?'

'Yes, indeed. Turns out she's well pleased you're back in town. She's going to ask you out for a meal this week.'

'I'm flattered.'

I finished the fizzy pop and crushed the can. I could feel a sense of resignation washing over me. Drowning me. And, you know, I quite liked it too. Maybe it was time to leave the past behind. To move on.

THE SEVENTH PART

There had been times when I wished I believed in something. Had a religion, maybe. I'd seen the Catholics clutching their beads and mumbling their mumbo jumbo but it had no impact on me other than creating a feeling of contempt. Scorn. Superiority. I knew that life was only a brief crack of light between two dark voids, after all. Only an idiot could think otherwise. Usually. But now, well, I knew I wasn't in hell but it wasn't far off, that was for sure.

Drella was just as surely dead. The slash across his throat was redder than his lips. And Sniffy had been beaten up to such a state he was almost unrecognizable. He was still alive, albeit barely. The Cobble Bar had been trashed, too. Still, they were all a sight for sore eyes compared to Scarecrow. His face had been stitched together until he looked like an explosion in a zipper factory. And he was most certainly alive.

As were the two leather-clad meatheads that stood beside him. Scarecrow had a hip flask containing liquid morphine and he was drinking it through a straw. Apparently, he was having problems speaking. He wasn't the only one.

'I told you that you were a has-been,' rasped Scarecrow. His voice was like broken glass. 'The old Tommy Bennett would have made sure I was dead and got rid of the evidence. But you rushed the job and got sloppy. It took me a while, but I got out of that grave you dumped me in. And look at me now. As good as new. Ha. Ha. Ha.'

He started coughing, took out a handkerchief and spat into it.

I might have forced a grin but the biggest meathead had made short shrift of my jaw. I couldn't say a thing and I couldn't move. I'd taken a beating and was slumped in the oak and leather armchair like an insect trapped in amber.

I'd received a phone call from Sniffy telling me to get down to The Cobble Bar sharpish and when I'd arrived I'd been confronted with this horror show.

'So, Tommy. Since you can't ask I'll tell you what I want. I only want your pain. And then death. These two big boys are John and Paul. And I kid you not, they have two brothers called George and Ringo. George and Ringo have gone to collect your mother, bring her here. When they come we will torture her. And then kill her. And then torture and kill you. We will get your daughter and granddaughter and the rest of your family at a later date but we will get them.'

I struggled to get out of the chair.

'Don't worry. We're not perverts but we are bastards,' said Scarecrow.

'I dunno,' said John, or Paul. 'Our George is a bit iffy. I wouldn't leave him alone with your Jack Russell.'

The brothers started to guffaw.

'Shut the fuck up,' said Scarecrow. 'This is serious.'

There was a loud bang.

'What the fuck is that?' said Scarecrow, he took out his handkerchief and spat into it.

Everyone was silent. Someone knocked on the front door.

'Who the fuck is that?' said Scarecrow.

He took a swig from his hip flask.

The brothers shrugged.

'Well, answer it then,' said Scarecrow.

The brothers went over to the door and as one of them touched the handle, the door exploded and the brothers were blown back into Scarecrow. They all collapsed into a heap on the ground. The room filled with smoke. Bev Ferry walked into the room wearing a WW2 gas mask and carrying a sawn-off shotgun. Two behemoths wearing woolly hats followed her in and started battering John and Paul with baseball bats as they struggled to get to their feet.

Bev took off the gas mask. She pointed the gun at Scarecrow.

'Is he the twat that sent them no-necks to interrupt your mother's bingo night?' she said.

I nodded.

Bev blasted Scarecrow's face off.

'That soft southern twat didn't realise who taught you everything you know,' said my mother as she walked into the room, dressed as Madonna. She had a Luger in her hand. 'They didn't know I had Bev on speed dial, that's for sure.'

Bev reloaded and shot John and Paul, yawning as she did it.

'Right,' she said, putting down the gun and nodding towards the two behemoths. 'You two can clear this bloody mess up. And don't forget about those two daft arseholes in the boot of the car. Dump it in the sea with them all in it. Okay?'

The behemoths nodded.

'Yes, Miss Beverley,' said one of them, his West Country accent purring like a tractor.

'I'll be off then,' said my mother, putting the gun in her glittery, gold handbag. 'I've got karaoke to get back to. I suppose I'll have to get a bloody taxi and they cost a fortune at weekends.'

'I'll take you,' said Bev. 'Your son can help these two clear up the mess. *His* mess, I should add. Okay?'

She pointed a finger at me.

'Okay,' I mumbled.

Mother turned to me.

'And make sure everyone's properly dead this time before you piss off, Son, eh?' she said.

I grunted my approval.

'Welcome home,' said my mother.

'You're welcome to it,' I said. Or at least I tried to.

The inky-black night had melted into a grubby-grey autumn morning. A pair of screeching, emaciated seagulls cut through the granite sky and landed on the rusty metal railings that lined the wet promenade. They stared at me for a moment before they took off and swooped down on the Rorschach test of blood and gunk that had splatted the statue of Colonel William Wainwright.

Colonel Wainwright, I vaguely remembered from my childhood, had been a local hero once upon a time. He had fought in the Crimean War or maybe the Boer War. Whatever, a hero, from an era when the world had heroes.

Now, his statue was covered in graffiti. Stained with piss and vomit. Discarded kebabs at its feet. A jagged crack running through its torso. A pink jester's hat on the head. Wainwright's statue was a soiled relic of a glorious past. I knew how he felt.

I looked away in disgust as the birds tucked in. My stomach still hadn't settled. It was just after dawn and everywhere was deserted. Out at sea, a lone fishing boat, adorned with fairy lights, rocked on the waves. It was over a month since 'The Cobble Bar Siege', as *The Seatown Mail* had referred to it, but I was still aching. Luckily, Bev's connections managed to cover the whole thing up and get the press and police to put it down to terrorists.

Soaked by the early morning sea spray, I fastened my black overcoat tightly. The cold autumn wind blew hard, and I pulled a flat cap from my pocket, put it on my head, and set off along the promenade.

My phone buzzed in my pocket. I took it out and looked at the screen. A text from Magda Nowak asking me how I was. I sat down on a wet bench and replied: Better and better.

The phone buzzed again.

Magda: Staying in Seatown for long?

I replied I had no plans to return to London in the near future. Her next message was about the ghosts I'd been seeing. I laughed to myself as I replied and told her that the ghosts had disappeared as soon as I arrived in Seatown. I was going to add an 'however' but thought better of it.

I got up and took a shortcut across the muddy town moor, the rain now attacking me from all sides. I jolted alert, a hand immediately on the pistol in my coat pocket, as I noticed a woman dressed in black on the path watching me. Her head was down and she was listening to an old pink Sony Walkman.

Our eyes locked for a moment as I walked past and I saw the eyes of the dead girl I'd shot in Garry Beachwell's driveway. She grinned and a shiver sliced through me. I watched as she walked off and disappeared down the cobblestone alleyway that led up to St Hilda's church. She stopped at the church gate and turned back to look at me. The graveyard was now full of more figures dressed in black. Scarecrow, Bernie Clarke, Gary Beachwell and lots of faces I didn't recognise. I knew those spectres would be with me to my dying days now. Maybe some parts of your past you could never escape. Maybe you never should.

I limped towards the bus terminus feeling ever older with each step but also with a sense of resignation, like before the break of a fearsome storm.

Paul D. Brazill was born in England and lives in Poland. His writing has been translated into Italian, Finnish, Polish, German and Slovene. He has had writing published in various magazines and anthologies, including The Mammoth Books of Best British Crime.

PaulDBrazill.com

On the following pages are a few
more great titles from the
Down & Out Books publishing family.

For a complete list of books and to
sign up for our newsletter,
go to DownAndOutBooks.com.

Exacting Justice
The De La Cruz Case Files
TG Wolff

Down & Out Books
March 2018
978-1-946502-50-6

Assigned the case of a gruesome—and very public—series of murders is Cleveland Homicide Detective Jesus De La Cruz, a former undercover narcotics cop and a recovering alcoholic. The cost of progress is more than he bargained for. Demands from his superiors, grief of the victims' relatives, pressure from the public, and stress from his family quietly pull him apart. With no out, Cruz moves all in, putting his own head on the line to bait a killer.

Abnormal Man
Grant Jerkins

ABC Group Documentation,
an imprint of Down & Out Books
September 2016
978-1-943402-39-7

Chaos? Or fate? What brought you here? Were the choices yours, or did something outside of you conspire to bring you to this place? Because out in the woods, in a box buried in the ground, there is a little girl who has no hope of seeing the moon tonight. The moon has forsaken her. Because of you.

Nine Toes in the Grave
Eric Beetner

All Due Respect, an imprint of
Down & Out Books
December 2017
978-1-946502-84-1

Reese has tried to live a good, honest life. But life has other plans. From the boss's wife who wants him to do something terrible to the sleazebags trying to set him up, when things go downhill, they go fast and Reese finds himself fighting for his life as the hard luck piles on.

His only way out might be to throw away the moral code he's been living by, face trouble head on and prove you can only push a man so far before he pushes back—hard.

Ridgerunner
A Killer from the Hills Novel
Rusty Barnes

Shotgun Honey, an imprint of
Down & Out Books
October 2017
978-1-946502-47-6

Investigating a deer-poaching incident that lands him in deep trouble wildlife conservation officer Matt Rider finds himself at odds with members of the renegade Pittman family.

When a large sum of Pittman's drug money comes up missing, clan leader Soldier Pittman is convinced Rider stole it. Rider's instincts are to call on his trusted friends, but none of them imagine the lengths to which Soldier Pittman will go to get his drug money back.

98635420R00081

Made in the USA
Columbia, SC
29 June 2018